# and a bird sang

## DIANE BESTWICK

# DEDICATION

Dedicated to the women around the world who have no freedom or social status simply because they are women.

I wish to acknowledge the inner turmoil they endure as they challenge the external voices beating down their inner conscience to live their truth.

Shirley Chisholm, the late black congresswoman sums up this conflict in her words:

*The emotional, sexual and psychological stereotyping of females begins when the doctor says, "It's a girl!"*

BESTWICK

# ACKNOWLEDGMENTS

I would like to thank the people of China who befriended me and often hosted me in their homes. I was privileged to meet students, colleagues and citizens in a variety of locations during the eight years that I worked there. Many shared their stories and the stories of those they loved. Chinese people continually read my manuscript for authenticity. Although the names of people and places have been changed, the story line is based on the true stories as told to me by these people.

In particular I would like to thank my instructor, Steve Alcorn, my mentor Christine M. Knight, and Crystal Stranaghan, who coached me through the publishing process. As well I would like to thank: Pam, Swan, Lily, Fanny, Siewling, Paul, Stu, Ed, Crystal, Lyn, Nivi, Gemma, Lianne, Jean, Xinran, Jackie, Joshua, Gavin, Joy, Christine, Bobbin, Olive, Peggy, Sheila, Sally, Tina, Lynne, Helena, Elizabeth, Dawn, Jean, John, Johanne, Linnea, Peter, Norma, Thora, Alison, June, Iris, Penny, authors Katherine Gordon, and Lyn Hancock. Thanks also to the staff of Mr. Druitt library, New South Wales in Australia. In addition, I would like to thank my mom, my father and my late grandmother.

All of these people contributed in some way to the completed manuscript as well as provided words of encouragement.

# CHAPTER 1

The crowd broke up and made for the park's exit. Lei headed for the WC, not because she had to pee, but because she hoped to discover her menses was starting. She was too distracted to stay and watch the awards ceremony.

Lei was a week overdue and fearing the worst. She didn't have the necessary government-issued birth permit to have another child.

Lei bumped past several girls waiting in line for an empty space on the long open channel that served as the public toilet. She straddled the opening and squatted down, then moved to avoid a pile of feces below her. She covered her mouth and nose with a tissue. The abandoned, blood-stained pads in the trash can in front of her loomed before her eyes. If only she would be so lucky. Optimistically she was wearing a pad.

Tears instantly stung her eyes as she stared at her unstained pad. She peed, and wiped hard with her tissue in hopes of finding some blood. Finding none, she brushed her tears away on the sleeve of her blouse, stood up and adjusted her pants. Outside, she stopped a moment and washed her hands under the communal tap. The cold water mixed with the salt of her tears. A lone chickadee chirped in the blooming jacaranda tree nearby.

Lei headed away from the Dragon Boat rowers. She was planning to go to her university dormitory. She changed her mind and made a stop at the pharmacy with the intent to buy a pregnancy test. If she was pregnant, she needed to know.

She entered the pharmacy and made her way to the back of the shop where she found the shelf of stacked pregnancy tests.

"Is this a reliable one?" she asked the clerk that had followed her.

"I wouldn't know, I've never used one."

Embarrassed, Lei decided to take the one she was holding. "I'll try this one."

"Okay, that's fifty-five yuan." Lei gave the attendant sixty yuan and received the change in coins.

The attendant went back to her business of making herbal packets for individual needs. The counter was arrayed with piles of seahorses, antlers, flower blossoms and rough barks. Lei had a fleeting thought that she might have to come back to buy a herbal remedy to bring on her menses. She quickly left the shop.

The market vendors called out to her as she traversed the crowded street. "*Zong zi?*"

Festival goers clustered around the food stalls with outstretched arms, coins in their hands, ready to buy their first *zong zi,* to celebrate the Dragon Boat festival. The smell of the steamed pork filling wrapped in bamboo leaves tempted Lei.

Food can come later, she told herself, and continued to maneuver through the crowd. Many people were dressed in the elaborate costumes they would wear that night as they participated in the "Awakening of the Dragons". Red paint would be dabbed on the eyes of all the dragon boats, hoping that they might see their way to win the race. Mellifluous music from a Chinese lute filled the air in the spaces between the bursts of fireworks and the sound of drums being gonged. If only she could share their party mood.

Lei unlocked her dormitory door. Straight in front of her, hung over their bed, was the huge wedding photo of Yimin and herself. Her eyes paused a moment to reflect on their smiles and then glanced down to the night table where there was a picture of four year old Kai, running after his dragon kite.

Will Yimin still be smiling if I truly am pregnant? Lei shivered, flipped her short hair back, and stood up tall. A sign of "sucking it up," as her foreign friend Cezanne had told her.

I can face this fear and deal with it, she affirmed.

In the bathroom, Lei ripped open the plastic bag with the test in it. She positioned herself on the toilet and held the strip so she could pee on it.

The instructions said to wait five minutes for results.

Five minutes. What could she do? If she were a Christian like Cezanne, she guessed she would be praying to her God to make her results negative. Instead she found herself standing beside her tiny bronze Guan Yin in front of Kai's photo.

Guan Yin, the Buddhist goddess of fertility, brings

children and was said to also protect them. She and Yimin bought this statue when she was pregnant with Kai. Both sets of parents were happy when they saw it, except for her father who said it was all nonsense. He adhered to a strong atheist stance and felt everything could be managed by following the virtue of Ren in Confucius's teachings. Ren exemplifies the normal adult protective feelings for children.

Lei shook her head, causing her short hair to brush her cheeks. She gazed at the statue and willed herself not to be pregnant.

Three minutes passed. Four minutes. She stared at the paper strip. Seconds later the bold red print "pregnant" appeared.

Lei felt her heart pound endlessly against her ribcage like a mallet.

It must be wrong, she rationalized. She knew she had missed one birth control pill but she had immediately taken two pills when she remembered. It had happened before and she hadn't become pregnant. Why this time?

She felt sweat break out on her forehead and under her arms. It can't be. Oh, how did it happen?

There's no way we can keep this baby. Maybe I

should have let the doctor tie my tubes like he wanted to.

Yimin will never understand. He knows we can't afford the fine, and now I'm studying. My job is waiting.

She sat on the bed, a curl in her spine. Gone was the optimism she had felt while waiting for the test results.

I don't want another abortion, but I know that's what Yimin will tell me to do.

Lei heaved a sigh, resting her head in her hands.

Maybe the test is wrong. She moved with resolve, determined to find out if it could all be a mistake.

Lei locked her door and made her way down the long hallway of the dormitory. Laughter could be heard behind her neighbours' half-cracked door. She slipped quickly past the door, afraid they might see her and call her in to share in their festivities.

Out on the street again, she passed the beggar boy. The narrow street alongside her building was his permanent home. His twisted legs were arranged on the sidewalk in front of his lean upper body. His eyes met hers and they exchanged a smile. She must remember to give him some warm dumplings on her way back home. He knew she would do this and looked away as if embarrassed to know of her kindness.

How does someone end up like this? she thought. Who was his mother and where was she? Lei recalled last winter when the snow came and he was no longer there. Where had he gone? She had tried to speak to him once, but he was mute.

In front of the pharmacy again, she paused a moment. How could she do this without causing suspicion? Maybe she should wait and ask Cezanne to buy her another test.

Impulsively, she told herself she couldn't wait.

She entered the shop and silently found her way again to the aisle with the tests.

"Back again?"

Lei jumped when the attendant broke her concentration.

"Yes, the other one had the strips missing."

"You should have brought it back, we could have exchanged it."

"No, I think I will just buy another one. Maybe a more expensive one would be better?"

The attendant held up the biggest, most colourful box. "Try this one."

Lei paid for it and made her way to the door.

"Lei?" she heard the attendant call after her. "That is

your name isn't it? You teach in Cixi don't you?"

"Yes, how did you know?"

"My Auntie's son was in your class and she told me you were here studying at university. I saw you at his graduation ceremony in Cixi."

Lei felt the sweat under her arms. Would the girl know she already had a child? She turned to go.

"You forgot your change."

Lei returned for her change and headed again for the door.

"Good luck, Lei," the woman called.

Out on the street, Lei felt safe blending into the masses. Why couldn't she just be a woman buying a pregnancy test? Why did she have to feel her actions were always monitored? Would it always be like this? She recalled her mother telling her this kind of society had sprung into being during Mao's time, when neighbours and even family members were made to spy upon each other.

Now they can't let go of this behavior, she had said. The walls still have ears.

Shaking herself, like a snake shedding its skin, she made her way down the street, the bag with the pregnancy test held tight to her chest.

Lei was oblivious to the noise of the crowd as she made her way back. She silently begged the Christian God, let her not be pregnant.

She passed the beggar, leaving him to fend for himself. Back in her room, the result was the same. She threw the strip in the garbage. She stuffed tissue on top of both the tests, assuring that Yimin wouldn't discover them.

She flopped onto her bed, staring at the ceiling. She bit her thumbnail, chewing on the cuticle until it bled. As she looked at the blood, she thought, if only this was the blood from my menses. Returning to the toilet, she checked her pad once more.

It was the same.

What was she going to do?

She could return to another pharmacy and purchase some herbs that might bring on an abortion, but what if they didn't? She knew of some retarded and deformed babies in the orphanage where her mother volunteered. Her mother said their problems were the result of such herbs.

Dulled by her circumstances, Lei drifted into a fitful

sleep. A picture of Gang, the leader of the Family Planning Committee flashed before her closed eyes. It was as if Gang stood right before her at the end of the bed.

Gang's lopsided stance seemed to accentuate her bellowing voice. She pointed her forefinger directly at Lei's nose.

"Get rid of it," she said. "You did it once, now do it again."

The vision of a baby crying behind Gang made Lei reach out to soothe the baby but it faded away, followed by Gang and her Committee members.

Lei woke with a start. She couldn't breathe. Why couldn't she save the baby in her dream?

Lei refused to think of another abortion. It's not too late to save my baby. Her head felt like it would burst with the reality of her intent. She rolled over, face down on the bed, covered her head with her pillow and wept. She wished she were dead.

Later, when Yimin came home from work, he found her still on the bed but in a fetal position. He showered and then slipped into bed. He curled his naked body around hers. She felt his hot breath as he kissed her neck. She didn't respond.

In the short time she had been awake, she had decided not to tell him her dilemma. Not yet.

"Are you okay?"

"Yes," Lei replied. She was glad the room was dark and he couldn't see her tear-stained face. They had sex but she was like a wooden doll, barely moving with his rhythm.

Lei woke long before daybreak. She lay frozen in one spot, afraid to wake Yimin.

How can I tell him I don't want an abortion? This time I want to give life to the baby growing inside me.

Last time Lei had had an abortion. She had done her duty. She had the abortion at two months, as soon as they found out she was pregnant. But this time it was different. It felt like this pregnancy was meant to be.

Her head spun with questions. Was she really being given a chance to make a different decision? Was there another choice? How could she go against the law and the demand she was sure Yimin would make?

When Yimin stirred, she felt his penis erect against her hip. His hands started to caress her belly and breasts. He flicked on the light to glance at the clock. Just five a.m. She knew he was thinking of more sex before work.

"I can't," Lei said and moved away from him.

"There's plenty of time." He inched back again.

"We need to talk." She turned and faced him.

He propped himself up on one elbow. His eyes glistened from the light of dawn. His intense stare always made her feel like a rabbit in a trap.

"About what?"

"Me."

A look of confusion covered his face.

"I'm pregnant," she heard herself say in spite of her decision to not tell him.

"But I thought you were using the pills."

"I was, but I'm still pregnant. I used two tests from the pharmacy yesterday and they both read positive." Why had she bothered to hide them if she was going to tell him?

She couldn't bring herself to add that it was her fault.

He sat up and pulled the thin sheet over his nakedness. Lei felt him struggling with this new information. She rushed ahead.

"Couldn't we keep this baby? For Kai, so he won't be so lonely. We could pay the fine. We could use the money we have been saving to pay back your family for your education. Surely they will want another grandchild instead of the money."

Lei knew Yimin's family had made great sacrifices when they decided to send him to the university instead of his older brother who had struggled at school. Now it was Lei and Yimin's duty to pay them back. Despite that, Lei felt they would be happy with another grandson.

"That's not possible. I'm putting the money into their account every week. Kai is their number one grandson. Why would they need another one? There's not enough money anyway."

"We could ask them." She pleaded. "I'm sure my parents would help too."

"No, you know the law, Lei. We have to obey it."

"But we could ask them?"

"No, I won't ask them. Do you think they want us to lose our jobs?"

"We wouldn't lose our jobs if we paid the fine."

"We're not paying the fine. It's more than you can imagine, my salary and yours for a whole year. We don't have that kind of money. Besides, we can only afford to raise one child. You know that."

Silence filled the room.

Lei slipped from under the sheet like a lizard escaping from a trap. She headed for the bathroom. If she didn't move fast, she knew Yimin would be sure to insist she go to the abortion clinic that day.

"I won't have another abortion," Lei choked out through clenched teeth as she slammed the door behind her.

Once in the shower, she soaped up her pubic hair and washed her private parts. In spite of her rush, her mind drifted back in time to a different day, a day she willingly went to the abortion clinic. That day she was like a robot, doing what her family and her husband insisted. Everyone knew they must obey the one-child law for the Motherland to prosper.

Suddenly, the vision of the Neighbourhood Family Planning Committee flashed before her eyes. They looked exactly as they had on that fateful day. Gang was surrounded by her cadres. There was agreement in all their faces. Gang's voice rang clear in Lei's head.

"It's your duty," Gang said. Her voice resounded with malice as the small eyes behind the narrow slits radiated contempt.

"They should have put an IUD in you after Kai's birth

and Yimin should have been sterilized."

Lei remained silent. Why should she tell her that Yimin wouldn't go to the sterilization clinic? He thought he would lose his manhood if he underwent the sterilization surgery. As for herself, the doctor did put an IUD in her but it was inserted cockeyed and the pain was unbearable. She had bled for weeks. When she returned to the clinic for her compulsory monthly x-ray to be sure it was still embedded in her womb, the nurse called the doctor and he decided to remove it.

Once removed, he wanted to do a tubal ligation surgery right then but she told him she needed to get back to work and she promised she would go back another day.

"Use a condom or better yet, practice abstinence," were the doctor's last words.

Well, neither had worked and that's when Lei found herself pregnant just after Kai's second birthday. Knowing the law, she knew what was expected of her. She didn't question her obligation. She knew she must obey her husband, her parents and her country.

That was two years ago, but it felt like yesterday.

*****

Gang and her two Neighbourhood Committee members had marched her to the abortion clinic near her parents' home in Cixi. Gang led the way. The rhythm of Gang's strong leg followed by her limp leg was unmistakable. She dropped her hip and pushed with her foot to steer the other hip in the direction she was going. She used her long gangling arms to balance herself, their swing matching the movement with her legs. Gawkers moved aside, familiar with Gang's way of moving. Her two staff members ensured Lei was following by clasping their arms firmly around her waist and shoulders. Lei trudged down the cobblestone road, a resistant accomplice, unaware of her footsteps, her head bent and eyes downcast. She knew she must comply but she was afraid.

A little child cried out as she passed. The child's grandma balanced her on a hunched back, hands clasped beneath the child's bottom to support her. The grandma lowered her eyes, avoiding Lei's glance. She knew their destination.

Lei heard the male munia birds in the trees overhead. Their red heads shimmering like crystal glass, their low single notes pulled Lei from the pavement to the wide-open space above. That was as far as her freedom could go. She was doing what she knew she had to do. Chairman Mao created this overpopulation mess and now it was up to the masses to correct it.

I am a loyal citizen and I will do it, Lei affirmed, turning her gaze forward.

A rat ran across their path and scurried into a garbage pile swept to the side of the building. Useless air conditioners dripped from above; water pooled on the rubble below. An old woman crouched over the debris. She made separate piles around her of cardboard, plastic and leftover food. Her hands were embedded with grime and stains of putrefied food. She made no eye contact with the procession as it passed.

The small group entered the clinic building.

On the first floor, the One Child Policy poster decorated the door panel. Its black and white sequence of pictures showed a beaming child from birth to graduation, its parents like angels above their one glowing child, nurturing it through every step of its life. If only it were so simple, she remembered thinking.

They walked up the next flight of litter-strewn stairs.

The musty smell of incense filled her nostrils. She

reminded herself that it was only tissue they were going to vacuum out of her, not a real baby. Isn't that what the ads on the buses said when they displayed discounts for "student abortions"?

When they reached the third landing, Gang pushed the unmarked door open and headed for the reception counter. Lei covered her nose and mouth as the strong smell of chloroform choked her. A miasma like old newspapers, wet with mould, permeated the room.

The room was crowded with women. Some young ones were obviously with their husbands. They avoided eye contact with Lei. The ones with their mothers or women friends were silent, their pallor evidence of tears held back. The girls by themselves looked down, as if by not acknowledging Lei they themselves might not be truly there.

The nurse looked at Lei and called them forward. The nurse nodded to Gang. Then she looked at Lei and half-smiled, recognizing Lei as one of her son's teachers.

Lei bowed her head, shame filling her heart. If only she could run home. But who would let her stay? She must do this. It was her duty.

Gang held Lei's elbow firmly and pushed her forward

to the examination room. Lei felt perspiration in her armpits and fear in her gut.

The harsh light over the examination table was blinding compared to the dim light in the rest of the room.

Alone with the nurse, Lei resisted getting up on the table which was draped with a blood-stained sheet. When she capitulated, she felt the stainless steel slab beneath the thin sheet drain the heat from her body.

"Pull up your skirt and open your legs." The nurse held scissors, and a sharp razor blade, ready to shave Lei's pubic hair. There was no soap, no water, only the sound of the scissors as she cut the hair. She felt the sting of her skin as the hairs that were left resisted being scraped by the razor blade. Lei was determined not to cry.

The doctor arrived and mumbled through his mask, "It won't take long."

His speculum was forced into her vagina like a knife in a pig's throat. Her muscles clenched, resisting the entry to open her cervix. Her spine went numb, both legs limp. A pain shot to the top of her head. She no longer knew what was happening to her insides. Tears squeezed from her eyes as she bit her lip and dug her nails into her palms. She was determined not to call out. She could have had anesthetic but she had opted to save the fee.

"Tell her to wear a pad for a few days."

Finished, the doctor threw his blood stained gloves in the trash can. She felt a stream of fluid running down her legs as she slid off the table and fumbled to find her underpants. The nurse smeared the fresh blood stains on the floor with the sole of her once white oxfords. She handed Lei a thin sanitary pad.

"Is it a boy or a girl?" Lei whispered as she watched the nurse wrap up something in newspaper and throw it in the same bin the doctor used.

"Don't be silly, it isn't a baby yet," the nurse said as she dismissed Lei.

That time, Lei bled continuously for a week. Yimin avoided her and colleagues enquired why she was away from duty so long. She told them her relatives from Inner Mongolia were visiting and as it was a once in a lifetime visit she had to be home to host them. She knew they guessed the truth but it wasn't something they shared. It was Lei's responsibility to correct the accident and that is what she had done.

When the bleeding didn't stop, her mother-in-law insisted she go back to the clinic.

This time they caught a cab. Her mother-in-law told the nurse of Lei's weakening state and they immediately had her up on the same blood-stained table. Ironically, the attending nurse who had ridiculed her previously, told her almost tenderly that the reason she was bleeding was because the doctor had left part of the baby inside. The truth of that statement had haunted her ever since.

That was two years ago. Life eventually settled back to normal, except she never forgot what she had done.

# CHAPTER 2

It had been two weeks since Yimin found out Lei was pregnant. The Dragon Boat festivities were over. Yimin was absent most of the time, sleeping in his dormitory at the ball-bearing factory some two hours away from Lei's dormitory. As a factory foreman it was expected that he would keep constant vigilance on almost every shift, a task that of course was impossible.

"Will you be here this weekend?" Lei asked Yimin.

Lei balanced her mobile on her shoulder while shifting books on her desk.

"No, you go see Kai yourself, Lei. I have to work overtime."

Lei imagined Yimin at his office desk, his suit jacket off, his sleeves rolled up and his slender hands sorting papers. His short cropped hair, tousled in spite of its length, would be moist from the heat of the day.

Yimin was tall and slim from his years of Qigong discipline. Lei had been drawn to him by his physique. There was something about how he held himself so erect.

His high cheek bones and intense black eyes also set him apart in Zhejiang province, his look characteristic more of northern Chinese people from Inner Mongolia. He had a way of looking directly at you when he spoke which was not common for most Chinese.

"Go Sunday before noon, Lei," Yimin continued. "Mama expects you. Everyone will be there for my brother's return from his holiday. They know I have to work. You take the bus, and I'll come later on my bike."

Lei clicked off the phone. She wondered if Yimin had any idea how hard this weekend was going to be for her. She was back at Shanghai University, having left her teaching career while she studied for her Masters degree in English. She had three assignments due on Monday, plus classes to attend all day Saturday. How could she manage to be free on Sunday? She had hoped that Yimin could go visit his family this weekend or at least they could go together and try to find time to talk about her pregnancy. She still wanted to convince Yimin that there must be some way to keep this baby.

She knew Yimin was absorbed in his work and was waiting for her to "take care of it", as he had said on more than one occasion.

Time was running out. She counted each day as it passed. Close to two months, she told herself at night when she was in the nude. Her nipples were beginning to feel tender. The sensation reminded her of the satisfaction she had felt with Kai at her breast. She found herself on the internet looking at the development of a baby in the first months. This was something she hadn't done the last time. She discovered they had removed a developing embryo not just tissue. She was even more determined to keep this one.

If only Yimin wanted this baby, she thought. Her head ached with scenarios of how she could keep it and for how long, especially once it was born. She saw herself hiding in the countryside, alone, away from prying eyes. But how could she feed herself and protect the baby? What about Kai? She woke up crying in the night.

In spite of her classes and assignments due, Lei found herself heading for the bus station on Saturday morning.

The sun was obscured from view by the thick smog. She hailed a pedicab. The cool of the vinyl roof and side panels gave respite from the heat but not the humidity. She was very much aware of the sweat of the driver, just inches in front of her. The smell of fresh rubbish piles being swept together by the street vendors added to her nausea.

The driver turned and pointed at the bus station ahead. Lei nodded and prepared to find the fare. She paid him and headed into the congested building to buy her ticket to Xinglu village. The waiting room was like an anthill, transient workers lugging cases and bags from one area to another. There were long queues from the road to the many ticket booths inside.

"Head out the back right now lady. Your bus is just leaving."

The inside of the bus was no relief from the heat. Lei quickly sat on a small stool set in the aisle behind the driver, the only vacant spot. Both her legs had to rest on a pile of cartons and string bags. Music from someone's iPod blasted her from behind. She wondered how many people recognized the English words of "Yesterday" by the Beatles.

If only I could go back to "yesterday". If I'd

remembered my pills, we wouldn't have this problem. And maybe if I hadn't already had an abortion it would be easier. This time I don't want someone to tell me I can't keep my baby. I want it. I want to hold it, put it to my breast and nurture it. Tell it I'm sorry for getting rid of it before. A lump formed in her throat and she blinked back the welling tears.

"All my troubles seemed so far away" kept repeating itself in her head. The words don't fit me, she thought. My trouble is right here inside me. She smiled as she looked down at her flat belly. It's not you, Little One, she almost said aloud. It's me. I broke the law.

I have to find a way to convince Yimin and our families that you are meant to be born. I don't want to abort or hide you or give you away. I want to keep you for Kai and me. Surely my family will too. She furtively slid her hands under her loose blouse and caressed her lower abdomen as if to protect the precious beginning of life from harm. Give me time and I will find a way to keep you, she promised.

"Yesterday" played again, for about the third time. It took Lei back some seven years before. She was in Ningbo, where Yimin's factory was based. She was being introduced to his older brother Dageng and his wife Qing for the first time. Yimin's parents were in the kitchen preparing the dinner meal.

"Do you have a child?" Lei asked Qing, knowing they had been married for three years already.

"No," Qing answered softly, her eyes downcast.

"But we soon will have," said Dageng. "It will be a boy for sure. We will follow the family tradition and have the first son."

Qing had smiled shyly in agreement and then left the room to help her mother-in-law in the kitchen. That was seven years ago. They still had no child.

"You must wait for us to have a child before you have one," Dageng had told Yimin soon after they married.

"I don't want to wait," Lei had argued when she brought home the application to have a child after a year of marriage.

"We will wait another six months and then my brother may have a son. If not, we will apply," Yimin said.

"You should have waited longer," his parents told them when they announced Lei was expecting. They hid their pleasure until Lei proudly gave birth to their first grandson. That day they announced to everyone the Yu lineage would continue, handing out red envelopes for family and friends to fill.

Lei's mother-in-law continued to harass Dageng and Qing.

"You are a Miao woman from Hainan," she told Qing as if Qing didn't know her own birthplace. "You are allowed to have as many babies as you want. Why don't you get started?" There had been silence.

Her mother-in-law didn't wait for an answer. She spoke into the air herself. "It's because Dageng worked too hard to send Yimin to university. Now he still works too hard. He has no time to make babies."

Lei hid her embarrassment. She knew her brother-in-law had made a great sacrifice to help his father on the farm. With the farm's earnings they had been able to support the younger brother at university. Everyone knew that her in-laws had been allowed to have two children because their first son was slow to develop and unable to master academic subjects.

When Kai was born, Yimin had held up his nude son, announcing that this baby would bring pleasure to all of the family. Kai had wriggled as his father proudly showed his genitals.

Qing had rescued Kai from his father, wrapping him tenderly in a baby blanket. From the moment of his birth, she insisted on holding him.

"He is my son," Lei announced one day when Qing again insisted on holding him all the time.

"Your turn will come," she had added compassionately.

A tear had fallen from Qing's eye. Seeing the tear, Lei had decided it was time to share her concern about Qing's inability to get pregnant. "Come with me to a clinic in Shanghai. I know they can help you."

"I will go, but I will go alone," Qing had whispered. "Dageng doesn't want me to talk to anyone. He says it's my fault. If I go, please don't tell him."

They could find nothing wrong with her. That left Dageng's fertility in question but of course he would never admit that possibility.

That was four years ago and still no baby.

*****

How can I tell the family I am pregnant again? thought Lei. It is sure to further alienate Dageng and Qing. Lei chewed on the inside of her cheek. The taste of blood brought her thoughts back to the present.

How was she going to gain her family's approval? She knew that her first duty was to her husband and her parents. Didn't Confucius say be mindful of your husband and elders and then a right society would be formed? But how could a right society be built on killing babies just because there were too many? Couldn't some other law help society? Surely the new babies are the ones that will respect and support their elders. Lei reflected on the reports she had read about too many boys being born and no girls for them to marry. The report questioned how this one child was going to support two sets of parents as well as pay for his own child's education when he did marry, if he could find a wife.

# CHAPTER 3

"You have to," Yimin repeated when he found out Lei still hadn't gone to the abortion clinic. He sat up in bed. His black eyes bored into Lei's and he demanded she listen.

Lei heard the other students' doors close as they left their dormitory rooms to attend their first classes.

This was Yimin's first day off from the factory since they had spoken about her pregnancy.

"Don't you understand? If you don't get rid of it, I'll lose my job and the men at my factory will lose their bonuses. You may never teach again. You did it before, why can't you do it again?"

The sting of his words penetrated Lei's heart where they merged with regret so deep she had to pretend it wasn't there. She imagined herself like an ostrich with its head in the sand.

"We have our son, isn't he enough?"

Stillness filled the room, as heavy as the weight Lei felt in her heart. She fought back tears. She wanted to tell Yimin about this precious life she sensed inside her, the life she didn't want to kill. Instead she remained silent, avoiding his eyes.

She stood up, ready to leave. He rose and stood blocking her way. He reached for her. She felt the squeeze of his fingers wrapped around both her forearms.

Why can't I just agree? she thought, as her heart pounded in fear. I know Yimin is right. But why can't I do it? As soon as she asked herself this question, she knew the answer. A day didn't go by she didn't remember some part of her first abortion and that it was she who had ended their baby's life. She had even figured out its projected birth date, and each year she burned incense at the temple of Guan Yin. She burned money and clothing on Qing Ming Day, the remembrance of the dead. Whether it was a boy or a girl didn't matter, but for Yimin's sake she imagined it had been another boy.

Her eyes glazed over as she stared at Yimin without

really seeing him. He released his grip. She watched as he sat on the edge of the bed and ran his slender hands through his hair.

She wanted to sit beside him and pull him back to her, let him hold her in his arms, comfort her. Maybe then she could tell him how important this baby was.

Minutes passed before she heard him repeat, "Do it."

He stood up and headed for the bathroom.

Lei lay alone, cold in spite of Yimin's body heat still left in the quilt.

He dressed and left without saying good-bye.

Lei heard his leather-soled shoes slapping the polished tiles as he headed down the long hallway to the stairway and out to their scooter parked below the window. She heard him undo the charging cord hanging down from the window. She imagined him buckling on his helmet and turning the ignition key, working his way out the front gates of the University and into the line of traffic.

Lei had moved to the middle of the bed, and curled herself up tight. She could smell Yimin's scent on the sheets. She pulled his pillow to her chest hugging it tightly. She knew she loved Yimin, but at that moment she hated him.

Why doesn't he understand? Why can't he take some

of the blame? I was using the pills so he didn't have to use a condom, she told herself. I heard on TV that the medical clinics are short of penicillin and other important supplies but their shelves are stacked with condoms. Why couldn't he use one? She stretched out, feeling her spine straighten. How am I going to justify my decision to our parents? No matter what I say, my father will tell me I have to obey my husband. I can hear him quoting the Chinese philosopher Confucius's two thousand, five-hundred-year-old teaching, only this time he will add the part about obeying our leaders.

Lei surmised that her mother would understand, but her in-laws were sure to remind her that Dageng and his wife were still childless. Why did they make it seem like it was Lei's fault Dageng and Qing hadn't done their duty and produced an heir?

Lei suddenly wondered why Chairman Mao created this monstrous situation. He was the one who told their parents to "make babies". What made him think China would be able to conquer the world with people rather than productivity?

Now I am being punished for his mistake, she thought. We are being told "less babies, more prosperity". What a contradiction. Who would create this prosperity, and who will enjoy it if there is no next generation? Her thoughts were interrupted by the chatter of voices outside her window. The break before the next class had already started. If she wanted to make her second class, she'd better hurry.

There was no water in the pipes when Lei turned on the taps for a shower. I hope there's some extra water in the water machine, she said to herself. Finding her water machine full, she put some in a basin and proceeded to sponge bathe, but when she turned to plug in her kettle she discovered there was no electricity either.

Yimin might return home, she realized. Last time they had been without electricity and water he had come home after he pressured his workers to be patient until the services came back on. His staff were migrant workers and would go where there was consistent work. They didn't like these "power-out days." They counted on long hours to build up their wages and bonuses for the Spring Festival holiday when they would travel great distances to return to their homeland with gifts and city foods.

Not wanting to face Yimin again, she decided to skip breakfast. She was, in any case, too nauseous to be hungry.

Unable to flush the toilet after she used it, she left the bathroom window open, hoping the breeze would minimize the smell. She gagged, vomiting on top of the feces. She dressed quickly, and left the room.

She hurried along the stone pathway to the Sociology Building. She gathered her baggy jacket around her body, avoiding eye contact with those she passed. Her internal dialogue continued. Why was she so helpless to protect the embryo inside of her? She thought with sympathy of mother turtles who had to lay their eggs in the sand and leave them to their fate. Well, I'm not a turtle, she affirmed as she entered the lecture hall.

The class had started. Dr. Xi was quoting Lu Xun, one of China's early satirical writers.

"Hope can neither be said to exist nor said not to exist. It is just like roads across the earth, for actually the earth had no roads to begin with, but when many people pass one way, a road is made."

These words resonated with Lei. She felt her burden lifted. She wasn't alone. It was as if every woman who wanted to keep her baby was with her, like an unseen force. It gave her hope. She felt power-filled.

This feeling lasted only a minute and then something evil pushed the powerful feeling away. Her mind pictured Gang and her committee members coming to get her. Lei was back on the abortion table. She was helpless.

The buzzer rang announcing the end of class. As she stood to leave, the blood drained from her head and she slumped down onto her seat. Her vision blurred and she felt like vomiting. Her classmate, Chao, placed her arm around Lei's waist and asked, "Are you okay?"

Later Lei lay wrapped in her quilt, tucked in by Chao and left alone to rest. How long can I keep this secret? she asked herself.

She dreaded seeing Yimin again. She still didn't have a plan. Maybe I should leave Yimin, but I know he would never let me take Kai. And where would we go?

Lei tossed and turned, still searching for an answer. She fell into a fitful sleep. A vision of a swimming carp appeared. The fish was leaping, doing its best to make its way up a steep waterfall. It tried again and again. In her dream she wanted to reach out and help it, place it in the calm pool out of the turbulence, but she was paralyzed. She wakened, feeling helpless. Disaster hovered.

Then she remembered the dream. The fish had been a golden carp. That was a good sign. A golden fish symbolized perseverance in a time of trouble. She didn't have an answer yet but she knew she wouldn't give up.

# CHAPTER 4

Gang climbed the four flights of stairs in the narrow building. Her good leg lifted as her weight shifted, then her shorter leg followed. The foot on her shorter leg was turned outward at an awkward angle. Except for her height and rounded shoulders, Gang looked like a toddler climbing the stairs.

She cleared her throat, coughed and spit the mucus on the landing.

The stairwell was filled with the pungent smell of frying garlic and the rhythm of cleavers chopping meat. At the top of the fourth landing, Gang used her key to open the door marked "Neighbourhood Family Planning Office." Three untidy desks were squeezed into the windowless room. Annoyed that her staff was late, she decided to sit at the first desk, ready to reprimand them on arrival. Gang drummed her fingers on the desk, her brow creased like a Shar-Pei.

Her cell phone rang.

"Where have you been?" her father demanded. "I've been calling you for hours."

Before she had a chance to reply, he continued, "You know the Central Committee is waiting for your quarterly report. Surely you can add up the number of pregnant women you have taken to the abortion clinic in this time. Are you understaffed or are you just incompetent?"

Again, before Gang could respond, he continued, "I never should have allowed your mother to talk me into giving you this position. You'd be better off on the streets as a prostitute."

Gang felt the vein in her neck start to pulse, a flush of anger suffused her face. Her two elderly co-workers had entered the room. They avoided her eyes and averted their heads. It was obvious they had heard her father's last accusation.

He continued, relentlessly, "I need those figures before Friday. Our funds from the Party depend on the total of the county's Family Planning results. We want to build a new hotel here in Cixi for businessmen coming from Shanghai. If the Central government doesn't give us the money, they will give it to Ningbo County and they will build the hotel. There's money in this project for me and your mother," he said in a conspiring tone. "Get those figures to my office now or your committee's salary will be nil, like yours."

He hung up. Gang snapped her cell phone closed and dropped it in her purse. She cleared her throat, and spat again on the floor. She fussed with her drinking bottle, shaking up the green tea leaves. Gang's short, cropped hair did nothing to hide the anger and contempt on her face. Her eyes darted back and forth from one employee to the other.

"Get to work," Gang demanded, her breath hissing through clenched teeth.

The workers stopped their tea drinking and pulled open drawers, feigning business. Gang headed for the door, the noise of her shuffling feet broke the silence in the room.

She smiled as she remembered her total admissions were already above her monthly quota. She just hadn't sent them to her father. Forcing those IUDs in so many post-menopausal women this month made sure of that. She gave a sort of snort as she recalled the women's concern that they really didn't need protection at their age. "Too bad," she had said. "We're going to give it to you."

He'll get those figures, she thought as she made her way, monkey-like down the stairs. I have the figures and I have one more to add to them.

The girl from the pharmacy in Ningbo had told Gang that Lei bought two pregnancy tests last week. If I can catch her when she is here in Cixi visiting her parents, her abortion will be added to my report, not Ningbo's, Gang thought triumphantly. And besides, it's payback time.

She headed out across the street, aware that people moved aside when they saw her.

Let Papa have his hotel, Mama her things that money can buy. I'll get my bonuses. One day they will be sorry.

Back in the present, Gang felt her hatred for Lei waken. "If she won't have another abortion, I'll double the fine." The hate rose up within her like a kundalini snake moving from its resting place at the base of her spine. Gang's mind rewound back to when she was at high school with Lei.

*****

"Place your finished papers on the desk upside down, and leave the classroom," said the adjudicator. Gang quickly slid the stolen exam from under her sweater and laid it atop the one she had been working on. Looking around to see that no one was watching, she slipped her own exam out from under the stolen one and pushed it up under her sweater.

Let's see Lei beat this mark, Gang said to herself as she limped out of the class.

"I don't believe it," Gang's father had said when she showed him her score. "How did you manage to get the top mark? Learning your own ways to cheat, are you?" She had sensed pride in his voice. But that happy moment hadn't lasted long. Her life was to change in a way she never would have anticipated.


She had met Bai at an intercity sports day, when she had been forced to sit apart from the participants because of her disability. It was her job to write down the scores the announcer was broadcasting.

"You not in any entry?" Bai had asked, unaware of her handicap as he stopped by the recording table to look at scores.

"No, I'm sick today," she had answered.

"Want me to help you?" Bai volunteered. "They are announcing the names pretty fast."

"Sure." Gang wasn't used to talking with boys. She was, and always would be, an outcast. The nearness of him confused her, but Gang heard her own voice speak up, "What school are you from?"

"The same as you, but I'm in the Sino-Canadian program. When I graduate I will go to America to study medicine. Want me to get us a drink?"

Gang bathed in the warmth of friendship. She knew his attention was because he hadn't seen her before and knew nothing of her deformity. They spent two hours that day getting to know each other. This was a totally new experience for Gang. "Don't play with her," she'd heard parents tell their children when her father finally managed to pay a primary school to accept her. "You might walk like that if you do." Even the teachers frowned upon any questions she asked.

"She should be kept at home," she heard the teachers

say to each other. It was the same throughout middle school, but always her father managed to pay for a spot for her. He didn't do it because he felt any closeness to her. If he had had his way, she would have been abandoned as soon as the hip deformity began to show itself. But it was too late then, her mother had already bonded with her and couldn't bear to give her up. She swore to give Gang an education so that one day she could look after herself.

Bai returned to the table with the drink for Gang. She avoided getting up from her chair. She had to pee but didn't want Bai to discover her disability. They found much to talk about, sharing their love of the godfather of Chinese rock, Zang Tianshuo. His lyrics echoed the cries of children who had suffered disaster and abuse. They discussed Zang's recent jail sentence after he was involved in a fight where someone had been killed. "Life is unfair." Gang had said, but Bai refused to agree with her. His outlook on life was more positive than hers.

"Why don't you come to the English Corner on Sunday?" suggested Bai. "We meet in the park by the school and talk as much English as we can."

"But my English is too poor."

"Come next week. Your English will improve."

At the end of the day, Bai reiterated, "See you Sunday evening by the fountain in the park." He smiled warmly at Gang. He hadn't discovered her disability.

Gang reviewed every word of their conversation that evening. It was as if a whole new world had opened to her. A world where someone listened to her, valued her thoughts, and cared about her, wanted to know more about her. It was an afternoon she would go over again and again in her mind.

She never went to the English Corner, and it was months before she saw Bai again.

When it did happen, he came up behind her in the cafeteria and followed her to a table.

She was unaware that he had followed her until she felt his warm hand on her neck as he whispered, "You know I can fix your hip."

"How?" she found herself saying even though she was embarrassed he had found her out.

"I'm planning to go to Stanford Medical University next year."

"Really?" hope in her voice. "If that's true, why can't they fix me in China?"

"Beats me. But I will do it for you one day."

From then on, they met at lunch and in the evening for study sessions. Bai was totally unfazed by her monkey-like walk. Their friendship developed from secret hand-holding, to stolen kisses, to eventually having sex in an empty book room after study hours.

"I'm planning to marry you anyway," Bai argued. "It's not like we're doing anything bad."

Because Gang didn't have any close girlfriends, she didn't know whether other girls were submitting to their "friends". She did know that boyfriends were forbidden until after university.

And then came the time that Gang would never forget. Lei had spotted Gang and Bai coming out of the paper room one night when they should have both been in their dormitories. From Lei's shocked expression, it was clear she knew they had been doing more than holding hands. The next day, Gang was called to the principal's office and told that only because her marks were high, and would help the school's status in the allocation of top schools in Beijing, was he allowing her to stay on at school until the end of the term. He refrained from telling her parents what he knew, afraid that they would pull her out of the school. But Bai's parents were told he was frequently seen with Gang. The principal knew this would be enough to have them forbid Bai seeing Gang again.

When confronted by his parents, Bai naively told them of his future plans to marry Gang and correct her deformity.

"You will never see her again," his father declared.

"It's hereditary you know," said his mother.

"That's not true. I have checked on the internet and it can be corrected."

"We didn't spend all our money educating you, Bai, to have you one day marry an invalid. Don't see her again. We already have plans for your marriage."

Bai tried to convince Gang that he would be faithful to her and marry her in America if she could just get herself there. But every word he said just made it clearer that there was no hope. "They won't let us see each other," he said, tears clouding his eyes. "They called you a cripple."

She's a cripple, she's a cripple, she's a cripple. The words echoed in Gang's head for weeks afterward. And every time she saw Lei, she was reminded who was responsible for her misery. High school had only been bearable while she had the love of Bai. And now she had nothing.

When Bai left to attend summer school at Stanford University, he was unaware of the consequences of their intimacy. So was Gang.

Two months later and still heartbroken, Gang had spent the whole day vomiting while she and her mother packed her things to go to Shanghai University. She had asked to go overseas to study, but they wouldn't consider spending the money.

When she continued vomiting, her mother insisted, "Come, let's take you to the doctor. I'm sure you have picked up the flu. The doctor will order an antibiotic shot for you."

At the clinic, her mother waited while Gang went in alone with the nurse and doctor. Fifteen minutes later, the doctor stood at the consulting door. Gang was red faced, holding back her tears.

"Your daughter is pregnant," he announced loudly. "Take her to the Family Planning Clinic immediately."

"It can't be," her mother gasped, shame welling up from within her.

They left the building in silence. Gang continued to vomit on the side of the street.

"Tell me how it happened," her mother demanded as she lead them both into the shadows of the building.

After hearing Gang's story of what she interpreted as seduction, she insisted, "Leave this to me. I will speak to your father."

"Send her away," is what her father said. He wanted nothing to do with his daughter or the forthcoming baby.

"But it will be our grandson. It will bring us great pleasure."

Finally her father agreed that she could go to her mother's sister's house in the countryside and wait there till the birth. He wanted nothing to do with confronting Bai. He knew Bai's family would by now have forbidden him to ever see her again.

Seven months later the baby was born. It was a boy, but it had a harelip. When they put it to her breast to suckle, it couldn't hold on. Both mother and baby cried. She would never forget the brightness in his eyes as he felt the warmth of her swollen breast and smelled the waiting milk. After the nurse had taken him away, Gang had tried to cut her wrists with the metal nail file she had in her purse. The nurse had returned without the baby, in time to condemn her for her actions and bind her wrists tightly. When Gang's mother came to get her, it was as if nothing had happened. They never discussed what had happened to her beautiful little boy.

Gang returned to Cixi. Her father avoided her, but insisted she take the job at the Family Planning Office.

"Forget university. It's time you contributed some money to your mother and me. We've spent years educating you, and for what?"

Well, contribute she had, but one day they would regret it. One day she planned to find her son and Bai. If Bai could fix her hip, she was sure he could fix their child's harelip too.

Today, foremost in her mind was finding Lei. Without her interference, Gang and Bai might have been living together happily in America.

# CHAPTER 5

"Stand with your weight on both feet. Put your hands on hips. Move your weight to the right leg, lifting your left leg up off the ground, bending it at the knee. Now pull your left leg back a bit, point the toe and kick, extending the leg and foot forward. Pull your leg back a bit and extend your toes up and forward. Lead with your heel. Kick this leg into the air. Now rotate your foot three times clockwise and then three times counter-clockwise. Do this three more times. Right, now lower the left leg and do the whole sequence with the right leg. Finish by placing your right leg on the floor and your hands by your side. You should feel a pleasing release of energy at the end of this form. Remember, release the negative when you kick; hold onto the positive."

Teacher Hu finished demonstrating "The Release" which closed the Qigong session. The class had been two hours long. Ian headed for the shower room. He was soaked with sweat. Yimin hung back, accepting a call on his cell.

"I know, Suzette, but I'm not free tonight. Don't call me on my mobile. I'll call you."

Yimin joined Ian in the shower room. They were both in their early thirties, but China's privations had taken their toll on Yimin.

Yimin's posture was slightly stooped, with round shoulders from years of study and no time for sports. Even his Qigong routines couldn't compete with his work load. When he added his glasses, he looked ten years older than Ian. Ian was American, well-muscled, fit looking. He had studied Qigong for fifteen years in California. He had wanted to come to China to study the special Zhineng Qigong, a type of healing with movement and sounds.

When the American offshore insurance company that Ian worked for decided to underwrite and protect ships in the South China Sea, Ian seized the opportunity to manage the Chinese operations so that he would be close to the Zhineng Masters. He was right in the heart of Asian martial arts, attending classes at the Shaolin Temple.

That was five years ago. Now he was also using a part-time job as a waiter and his Qigong study as cover. So far it had worked. Not even his girlfriend, Cezanne knew about his real job. Being undercover was important if he was to protect his company's ships in the South China Sea. Modern day pirates were ruthless in their pursuit of what they considered theirs. A ship could be safe one day and hijacked the next.

Ian was in constant radio contact with his head office in the States as well as their ships in the area. Taking these calls on his wireless radio away from Chinese censors was a part of the job, as was drinking and night-clubbing in places where informants hung out.

"Your wedding anniversary must be coming up Yimin?" Ian asked as he dried himself with his towel. "I remember your wedding well. Cezanne designed the white wedding dress for Lei. 'One of a kind,' she said."

"Best forget the anniversary this year," Yimin responded as he used his small Asian towel to dry off.

"Why do you say that?"

"Lei and I are not agreeing right now. She wants another baby. I don't."

"But I thought you couldn't anyway. Isn't it the law?"

"Too late, she's already pregnant," he said with resigned certainty.

"God, what are you going to do?"

"I want her to get rid of it but she won't. We may have to move."

"What do you mean move? Wouldn't they find you?"

"Sometimes yes, sometimes no. Didn't you see that recent Chinese New Year's skit on the television? They told of all the population guerrillas who move from province to province hiding their next child." He gave a forced laugh as he recalled the skit, though obviously the reality of the situation was too close to his own.

"Escaping's not really an option. I mean Lei's studying now and we couldn't leave Kai."

Yimin's phone rang again. He glanced at the caller ID and closed it. His frown made Ian ask, "A problem?"

"Another one, but more complicated."

"You want to talk about it?" Ian's tone was personal, their five years of friendship bridging the gap between cultures.

Yimin coughed, looking around to check that they were alone. "You know I've been hanging out with a young crowd after work. I've seen you and Cezanne at some of the clubs. Lately the 'mother-in-laws' are moving in closer for their protection money from our factory. I've been gambling a bit and drinking with some of them, hoping they might back off, but no luck. Our owner has just so much cash he can use for this kind of thing."

"So, are they pressuring you for more?"

"No, but one of their girls is. She wants more of my time than I have to give."

"Shit, Yimin. I didn't think you believed in all this mistress stuff. What will Lei do if she finds out?"

"I can handle Lei. It's this young doll I have to get off my back."

"Yimin, do you hear yourself? You're taking a very big risk of losing Lei and Kai if she ever finds out. Lei's not the average Chinese woman. She might even divorce you. But then maybe not if she's pregnant like you say. At any rate, it's too dangerous, Yimin." Ian had stopped getting dressed and stood staring directly at Yimin. "Don't think you can be friends with these gangsters, male or female. You can't. I know that."

# CHAPTER 6

It was raining, but not hard enough to wash the smog out of the air. It was impossible to breathe freely. Many pedestrians wore cotton masks in an attempt to filter the foulness.

Lei paced up and down in her dormitory room. Her books were piled on the floor around her. She adjusted a few of them from one pile to the other. Her elbow knocked over her mug of green tea which she had carelessly left on top of some papers on her desk.

"*Bai chi,*" she cursed. You idiot.

Frustrated with herself, Lei decided to visit Kai again.

It had been a week since she was at her mother-in-law's home. That was the Sunday Dageng and his wife, Qing, returned from their holiday.

She remembered thinking, This baby should be in your womb, Qing. First because it's past time for you and Dageng to be having a baby and second, because you, like my mother-in-law, are a citizen of one of China's minority groups. You can have as many children as you want.

She remembered the jolt she got when her thoughts were interrupted by her mother-in-law. It was as if she were reading her mind until she realized she was addressing Qing.

"You give me grandsons yet?"

Qing, as always, got very shy and busied herself whenever her mother-in-law reminded her that she had failed in her duty to have the first grandchild.

"Not yet, Mama," Dageng responded for his wife.

They all knew that Qing had subjected herself to acupuncture, herbal potions and cupping of glass bottles on her skin to induce fertility, all to no avail. Only Lei knew about the visit to the clinic in Shanghai.

Lei hoped that the holiday would have helped. It was the first time that Qing had seen her parents since getting married seven years earlier. Lei half expected her to bring back a child from one of her sisters and declare it their own. It seemed they were too proud for that.

Against all logic, Lei was beginning to think more positively this week. Her guilt was beginning to be replaced by a kind of fatalistic belief.

Janine, her zoology lab partner, and Lei had twice walked past the small Daoist Jing Yan Temple on campus. Janine commented that Daoist believers burn incense on the first and fifth days of the month to remember the earth Spirit Jiang Ziwan who blesses the birth of babies into families. It comforted Lei to think that this Spirit, like her Buddhist one at home, might be on her side.

Deliberating, Lei considered, I'm not Buddhist or Daoist, but I feel a strong desire to burn some incense myself. Why do I feel soothed by the knowledge of the belief? Intellectually I know there is no proof. She remembered something her Qigong instructor had said: "Stop analyzing and breathe."

Maybe I can keep this baby myself. I could finish this semester and then take a break to have the baby. I could study my courses on-line like I have seen Cezanne do. I will ask her to advise me. I feel I can trust her with my deepest feelings. When I return from my in-law's home, I will ask her.

Lei headed for the bus depot. It was chaotic with tourists and locals alike. Double-decker buses lined the compound, offering tours of the famous Oriental Pearl Television Tower, the Jade Buddha Temple, the Bund and the People's Square.

She managed to find the express bus and was soon out of the city limits and into the flat plains land. Apartment buildings and factories were left behind. The sky cleared of its grey cover and the sun shone uninterrupted on the fields lining both sides of the highway. When she opened the window she could smell the scent of the blossoms. Orchards of peach trees dotted the landscape, their boughs lacy with bursting buds. Rice fields were planted with their second crop of seedlings.

The aroma of noodles and vegetables steamed together engulfed Lei as she stepped from the bus at the crossroads where her in-laws lived. Freshly cut pineapples were skewered on sticks and small candied fruits were stacked on bamboo twigs. The smell of popcorn added its essence to the morning air.

Lei walked the five-minute route along the canal to her in-law's compound. The compound was sandwiched between two small shops. Suddenly she heard Kai's laughter.

She unlocked the iron gate enclosing her mother-in-law's property. In the concrete paved yard, near the open well, Qing was crouching by the water pump, plucking a freshly killed duck, its head hanging at a strange angle. A turtle, about the same size as the duck, swam in a basin, unaware that it was next.

Qing nodded to her. A smile on her face. She knew that Lei's chief reason for visiting was to see Kai.

Kai rushed to her arms, squealing as she hugged him and swung him around.

"Look at my lizards," he said as he showed them to her. His grandfather had banded some mosquito netting over the top of the opening in a short section of bamboo to keep them trapped.

"I want to catch more. Maybe a whole family of lizards."

"Of course you do."

She nuzzled her face in his small neck, inhaling the smell of moist skin. How she wanted to tell him about the possibility of a new baby brother or sister. Instead, she removed the warm tiger hat he was wearing. The bright orange and black fabric accentuated the flush of his cheeks. The country folk believed these tiger hats would keep the evil spirits away from little ones. His head was wet with perspiration.

The smell of hot roasting peanuts drifted out of the lean-to room attached to the main two-storey stone building. Kai led her to the shed.

They spotted her mother-in-law sitting on a low stool in front of the huge cast iron wok sunk in a homemade stove of tile and brick. She constantly stirred the raw peanuts in the salt and oil.

Her father-in-law was crouched down behind the wok, continually feeding dry twigs into the fire. "Sit down," he said. His weathered face was shiny and red from the heat of the coals; his body wizened but still sturdy. "We have been at this job all day. You would be proud of Kai, he has been gathering twigs to burn as well as shelling the peanuts for us." The floor was strewn with shells. In one corner of the shed the bicycle farm cart was parked. It was still loaded with vegetables from their land.

"Come and we will prepare the meal," said her mother-in-law. She handed her stirring stick to her husband. "Lei, take some fresh bok choy from the cart."

Outside at the open kitchen, Lei placed rice in a pot with

water from the courtyard well. She balanced the pot over a small coal burner, feeding as much coal as it would take to sufficiently boil the rice. She added some dried shrimp.

"Qing has gone to take some food to Dageng in the field. He is harvesting sugarcane today and won't be home till late. We will eat."

Kai chattered throughout the meal as Lei fed him and asked him questions about his day working with his grandparents. Her problem seemed so far away.

"Come on, Kai. Time for bed. Go get the bowl for the water."

Lei filled the basin with warm water from the thermos given to her by her mother- in-law.

"Take off your shoes now."

The suds turned into bubbles he could play with as she used the small face towel to wash his hands and feet. "One last wipe and you're finished." Lei caressed his face and neck with the damp cloth.

"Do you have to go, Mama?"

"Yes, sweetheart, you know Mama is studying at the University. Papa will come soon to see you."

She tucked him into the wooden framed bed beside his

grandparents' bed, being sure his quilt was wrapped snugly under and over him. The temperature had dropped from the daytime heat.

She lay with him awhile and told him stories about himself when he was a baby.

"Did Papa really lose me in the market?"

"Yes, but he found you sitting with the ice cream man. You had an ice cream cone for free."

Very soon he drifted off to sleep. She stroked his shiny black hair and ruddy cheeks before she kissed him one more time.

How had he grown so quickly in just four years?

When she glanced back before leaving the room, her heart was light. She had a feeling that everything was going to work out.

"This is heavy," she said as she lifted her pack. It was stuffed with fresh cucumbers, leafy bok choy and cut sugarcane.

"Here, take these too," her mother-in-law said as she tucked in a bag of warm peanuts on the top of everything. "These are for Yimin."

"Thanks." She zipped up her pack.

Her mother-in-law followed her to the gate.

"When are you going to do it?"

"What do you mean?"

"The abortion."

How did she know? Had Yimin told her? When had he had time to ride way out here? Her mouth went dry.

"I don't know," she whispered, avoiding eye contact.

"What do you mean you don't know? It should never have happened and now you must decide what you will do. As I see it, you have two options: obey the law so you and Yimin won't lose your jobs, or go in hiding and have the baby. If you do that, you can give it to Dageng and Qing. They have waited seven long years to give us a grandson."

The blood drained from Lei's face. Her hands went instinctively to her womb. How could she have this baby and then give it to Qing and Dageng? Before she had time to think more, her mother-in-law continued, "You must give it to your brother-in-law. Yimin has already agreed to this arrangement. You and Qing can go to her family on Hainan Island. You will be safe there. They will think you are one of them and can have as many children as you want."

Lei hadn't heard any of the words telling the rest of

her mother-in-law's plans. Her mind was still focused on Yimin's support for his mother's plan.

Lei wanted to run. Her heart felt stabbed. How could he have done this? He hadn't even found time to talk to her about how they could keep this baby.

She was too upset to speak. Out of respect for her mother-in-law she didn't answer. She had hoped her mother-in-law would understand how she felt about this new life inside her. After all, she had two sons.

As if she read Lei's mind, she said, "You are Han Chinese, Lei. I am not. You must obey the law or give it to Qing."

Lei still didn't answer. She was in shock. Such an option had never entered her head. This was her baby, she wanted it for herself and Kai. How could she give it away? Why hadn't Yimin told her of this plan?

Lei picked up her things to leave, shaking off her mother-in-law's grip. As she stepped away, she heard the angry warning, "If you don't do it, you'll bring shame on your husband's family."

When she got to her dormitory door, Lei discovered a small bag of cotton root bark in a brown bag hooked on her doorknob. Who had put it there? Yimin? Gang?

Whoever it was expected her to use it.

Was it that easy? Could she just drink something and it would all go away? What if it didn't work? She had seen deformed and mentally handicapped babies at the orphanage where her mother volunteered. It was said that they were this way from the effects of herbs their mothers had used to try to induce an abortion. She thought for a minute about Gang's baby. Is that what she had done? Her mother had told her which toddler was Gang's at the foster home where the owner took babies from the clinics and hospitals that would otherwise be left to die. Lei knew it was harder to find adoptive parents for children with deformities. Her mother had assured her though that they would one day find an overseas "forever family" as they called them, who would arrange for the necessary operations to correct his harelip. Gang knew nothing of this. It was a secret they shared.

She looked at the sinister bark in the palm of her hand. She walked determinedly to the bathroom, tipped them into the squat toilet, and flushed it twice to be rid of all the debris.

She scrubbed her hands till they were red.

## CHAPTER 7

Lei lay in bed, unable to sleep. She was still upset by her encounter with her mother-in-law.

The telephone in her dormitory room rang. Cezanne's cheerful voice greeted her. "Want to go for a pot of tea?"

"Sounds great," Lei said, putting extra effort into her words.

"Let's go to the Huxinting Tea House on Nanjing Road where Ian works. It shouldn't be too busy with the usual tourists. Take the bus and I'll meet you there in half an hour. I'm at the pool now. Bring your suit and we can start those swimming lessons I promised you, after our tea."

"Okay for the tea but a maybe for the swim," Lei said and hung up the phone.

Cezanne had talked with her about facing her fear of swimming and just "doing it", as she said. Well, learning to swim was not a priority right now. She couldn't even stand up to her mother-in-law, how could she face her fear of swimming? Lei wanted to talk about her situation.

During the night, she had dreamed about giving Qing her baby but Qing wouldn't take it. She said she wanted her own son. Her mother-in-law, Yimin and Dageng said she must take it, that she was never going to have a son.

Yimin had muttered to Qing, "You should never have aborted the girl baby you first carried in your womb."

Was that what had happened? Was this why Qing couldn't get pregnant?

Lei had woken up crying, clutching the picture of Kai she had fallen asleep with. What if she ever lost him? Thankfully they had known that he was not a girl in her womb. Would Yimin have asked her to abort it if it had been a girl? Confused, she looked to her meeting with Cezanne for support. She hoped Cezanne would be able to understand what it was like to be a Chinese wife.

She dressed and checked her purse for the one yuan she needed for the bus. It was Sunday morning and the streets were crowded with pedestrians and cars. People on motorcycles and bicycles wove in and out of the cars, often just missing each other like balls on a pool table. The crowd at the ticket window of the bus depot was huge. She slowly worked her way to the front of the throng.

"It's a long line," the pregnant woman behind her said, smiling.

"Yes. Here, you go in front of me."

Lei's spontaneous kindness had the effect of calming her. All might still be right in her world after all, she thought.

There must be a way for me to safely keep this baby. I just have to find the right way. Could giving it to Qing be the answer? She caressed her tummy, thinking of Qing's hardship without a child. She knew adoptions within families were an acceptable practice, but the children were generally not told of the arrangement. The adoptive families were afraid the child would not support them in old age if they found out the truth. They would feel an obligation to their true birth family and abandon their adoptive family. What would this child do?

As Lei sat on the crowded bus, heading for the crossroads between the New Economic Zone and

Nanjing Road, her heart filled with love for her friend Cezanne. They had both been at the University almost a year now. They had been friends for almost five years. Lei had been assigned to assist Cezanne when she first came to Lei's school as the grade ten English teacher from Canada. They had become friends immediately. Their common bond was the students. They were both committed to their students' achievement. Cezanne had come to understand how Chinese teachers felt for their pupils. They were their second mothers and would do almost anything to enhance the students' academic growth. They were still discussing how many teachers would even help their students to cheat. She knew that Lei was not one of those teachers. She put her students' achievement foremost in her teaching, but helping them cheat was not part of it.

Lei's heart gladdened at the thought that she would soon share her problem with her treasured friend.

"My stop," she called out as she pushed through the crowd on the bus, and descended the stairs to the congested street.

She found the gate to the Old City. This gate was the entrance to the old walled fishing village. Not much of the wall was left, only the gateway that one passed through to enter the new area. She could see the Chenghuang Temple ahead of her, surrounded by the Yu Garden.

The teahouse was connected to the temple by the Bridge of Nine Turns. The legend was that evil spirits have trouble with corners.

"Gone are all my troubles," she sang as she traversed the nine turns, rubbing her tummy gently.

She entered the restaurant, spotting Ian immediately.

"Hi Ian, seen Cezanne yet?"

"No, but I just came on shift, maybe she's sitting somewhere waiting for you."

They checked all the window seats where Ian knew they liked to sit.

"Don't worry, Ian. I will wait for her."

She settled into a small round table by the window and Ian left to attend to another customer.

The view down the Huangpu River was crowded with sailing vessels. Cruise ships, barges and freighters wound their way into this seaport. Cezanne had been fascinated when Lei had told her the Huangpu was joined by the Yangtze River which had its headwaters at the foot of Mt. Everest. Both rivers emptied here into the East

China Sea.

She saw Cezanne enter the restaurant, her long blond hair moved like a surfing wave, framing her oval face, alight with a smile, eyes sparkling. Cezanne greeted Ian with a hug and then she maneuvered her way between the crowded tables.

"I swear you carry sunshine with you wherever you go," Lei said as she greeted Cezanne with both hands. Cezanne's slim but feminine figure was accented by the teal green dress she loved to wear with matching silk pumps.

"Look at me," Lei said, gesturing to her baggy clothes and dark coat. "I forgot you always like to dress up when you come here."

Lei relaxed, absorbing the hug Cezanne gave her. She had learned to expect this style of greeting from Westerners.

Their tea arrived in a flat bellied glass pot. The waitress set it down on the wrought iron stand, and lit a small candle under it. Sliced strawberries, apples and tangerine oranges floated in the boiling water. A small black tea bag dangled in amongst the fruit. The waiter filled their miniature cups before he left them alone.

"How's Kai?"

"Great, Cezanne. He loves the English nursery rhyme book you gave him, especially 'Twinkle, Twinkle, Little Star'. He's learning that one at kindergarten. You should have seen him last time I went to pick him up. He knows all the actions to the songs, and he can say all the English words."

Lei added, "You know, Cezanne, Yimin's parents don't think he needs to go to kindergarten each afternoon, but thank goodness, Yimin supports my decision. It's an extra cost, but we both agree, he must learn English early if he is to compete in middle school one day."

Lei fell silent and Cezanne sensed she had something more important to share. When Lei spoke it was in a whisper.

"I'm pregnant, again."

Aware of listening ears, Cezanne shifted her chair to lean closer.

"And Yimin wants me to have an abortion or give it to my sister-in-law." Tears were forming as Cezanne handed her a serviette and moved even closer, her hand on Lei's shoulder this time.

"Are you sure you're pregnant?"

"Yes, I took two tests, and now I feel my breasts changing."

"What are you going to do?"

"I don't know. All I know is I want to keep it. I thought Yimin would understand and help me but he's just making me feel guiltier than I already feel." She looked around as if to check if anyone heard her. "It's my fault 'cause I forgot some of my birth control pills."

Cezanne drank her tea slowly and then put her cup down. Her eyes met Lei's and she started to speak. She changed her mind. Moments passed before she asked if she had Lei's permission to share something that might upset her. Confused but trusting, Lei nodded.

"Go ahead."

"I think Yimin is having an affair. Ian and I saw him at a night club in Ningbo with a young girl."

Lei's hand went to her mouth and she seemed to stop breathing. Her other hand instinctively went to her abdomen.

"It can't be," she managed to say.

Hating the impact of her words and wishing the truth was not so cruel, Cezanne answered, "We're sure of it. Ian spoke with him and we saw them leave together."

"Oh, Cezanne, you must be wrong," Lei repeated impulsively gathering up her purse and jacket. "I have to go and talk to him. It's the only way."

Cezanne understood that her friend had to confront the situation. She stood and signaled for the check. They left without saying good-bye to Ian. In the cab back to the dormitory Cezanne held Lei's hand and looked out the window. "Here's another tissue," Cezanne said as she passed one to Lei. Tears streamed down Lei's face.

Back in her room, Lei quickly gathered some things to spend the night in Ningbo. She headed for the bus depot. She knew it was late but all she could think was that she had to prove Cezanne wrong.

Her mind drifted. She was back in Xiamen, under the artificial starlit sky of the nightclub restaurant on their honeymoon.

"We'll dance all night," Yimin had said, and then he had ushered her away early to the honeymoon suite.

For the rest of the week they had danced till the early morning hours and then made love till midday. They were both virgins when they married, their lovemaking consisting of caresses and gentle penetration until it was no longer painful for Lei. She remembered collapsing in Yimin's arms the first time he had climaxed deep within her. She thought it was a bond between them. What had happened?

Lei had known that he was stressed about his work, but she had never questioned his faithfulness. Cezanne must be wrong.

The night watchman at Yimin's factory shone his flashlight on Lei's face. He knew it was unusual for her to arrive so late and alone. He recognized her as Yimin's wife and dutifully unlocked the gate.

"Be careful miss, it's dark down there."

She used her flashlight to find her way down the long hallway when she entered the dormitory. When she came to Yimin's door, she knocked determinedly.

She could see from the small window above the door that there was no light on. Yimin must still be in the factory. It was 11:30pm.

As she turned to leave and go find him, Yimin opened the door. His chest was bare, his hair wet and his sweat pants low on his hips. He had a wine bottle in his hand.

She was taken aback at first, not comprehending the situation. As light from the doorway spread across the room behind him, she saw movement in his bed.

"Why are you here?" Yimin demanded, his voice slurred and angry.

She pushed him aside and stepped into the small room, confronting the young girl who was standing now, attempting to gather her clothes.

"Get out," Lei screamed as the girl slipped on her coat to cover her body, her head turned to avoid Lei's gaze.

Yimin tried to stop the girl as she rushed past him and out the door. The door slammed. Yimin turned to Lei.

Her fists pounded on his bare chest as he reached to control her. "I hate you, I hate you!" she sobbed as Yimin grabbed her wrists and pushed her away. She stumbled and slumped down onto the tile floor. Looking up she saw Yimin throw back his head and take a long drink from the bottle.

In that short space of time, Lei asked herself a flood of questions. Her whole married life seemed to flash before her. Was this the man who had committed himself to her alone on their wedding day, the father of Kai and now this new life inside her? The life he was so willing to give away to his brother?

She rose, knowing she had to get out of there before

something worse happened. As she headed for the door she heard the bottle hit the full length mirror, smashing the glass. Broken dreams littered the floor.

Yimin grabbed her arm and spun her around. "Have you had the abortion yet?"

She felt her hand slap his face before she even planned it. The force of the impact raced up her arm, and exploded in her chest. She turned and ran out of the room, careening down the dark hallway.

"Don't leave me Lei!" she heard Yimin call out to her.

## CHAPTER 8

Alone on the bus going home, Lei remained in shock, until she realized her body was shaking uncontrollably. Past and present, dreams and reality blurred together. Was what she had experienced real? Was the other woman a nightmare? Did Yimin really push her? Her quiet sobs were masked by self-absorbed teenagers talking on their cell phones. She eventually fell into a fitful sleep.

Lei woke to the sound of the driver announcing that they were entering the outskirts of Shanghai. Her eyes were dry. Her pain too deep for tears.

Why had Yimin pursued another woman? Lei remembered the scent of the girl's long hair as she had brushed so quickly by her. Lei's hair had been cropped after she gave birth to Kai, as was the custom.

Yimin had not wanted her to cut her hair, but both mothers insisted. Tradition dictated that Lei was not allowed to wash her hair or shower for a month after giving birth. Chinese believe that a new mother must be totally inactive for thirty plus days. She must stay indoors, be bundled up in clothes and socks, even when it was hot outside. She was fed "confinement food"— tons of ginger, sesame oil, black vinegar and wine in every dish. All of this to keep her from getting "wind" on her body or inside her. It was a time for the mother's body to repair itself from the birth trauma.

Well, look what my obedience has done, thought Lei. I am no longer attractive to Yimin. Why else would he take a mistress. How can he be so deceitful? Her mind buzzed with questions. Who is she? A student? A worker from the factory? She barely looked twenty. What do I lack? Where did I go wrong? Why does he need a girlfriend? Suddenly she was sure the first unexpected pregnancy had something to do with it. He knew she had dutifully had an abortion but they never spoke about it. He waited till she indicated the pain and bleeding had stopped before he touched her again. There had always been a hesitation to their love making since then, as if he was 'asking' her if she wanted to do it. She thought maybe he had understood her pain and didn't want to cause it again.

But why was he drinking so much? He and his father had always loved their yellow wine made from the fragrant rice. They always drank it with their lunch and dinner meals when they were together. In the winter they drank it hot. On special occasions, such as weddings and Spring Festival meals, Yimin brought bottles of red wine, from Australia and New Zealand, preferring those to the local Chinese red wines. Now that he had the better factory job he could afford them.

A thought surfaced as she remembered he liked to drink beer with his factory workers after a long shift. Tsingtao beer, made in Quingdao, was his favourite. They all shouted *Ganbei* (bottoms up), continually throughout the meal as they toasted each other from across the table. He told me they like the original Tsingao slogan; "Drinking Tsingao beer can give you passion and happiness." Is that what he wants? Passion?

Lei looked down at her loose coat, cloth slippers and knapsack. She ran her hand through her unkempt hair and visualized her loose undergarments.

I have changed from when Yimin used to say he loved my long hair and slim body. My breasts are soft and I have a scar on my belly because the doctor insisted I have a caesarean delivery for Kai.

Lei tried to recall the last time they had sex. The restriction of their jobs and separate dormitory lives was a challenge. It was like that for all Chinese couples. Now that she was at university, it was even harder to find time together. Her mother told her that this was a plan set out by the Communist Party years ago. Intimacy and familiarity among couples was not encouraged.

Look what it has done to us, she lamented. It's made him take comfort with another woman. Despair enveloped her. Anger soon replaced it.

Her mind flashed to the many times she had arrived at Yimin's dormitory room and found him alone with his TV on and empty bottles on the floor beside the bed.

"Have you drunk them all yourself?" she had asked.

"What do you think?" he had laughed, pulling her down on the bed. The question was never answered. She had never anticipated the forewarning of something sinister or suspected another woman.

*****

The lights of Shanghai loomed ahead of the bus. Soon she would be home.

Home. Where is home? Our dormitories aren't home, she thought. I thought home was where Kai, Yimin and I would be together someday. Sometime in the future after we pay off Yimin's family and we all manage to save for our own apartment. Not a separate house as Cezanne told me westerners have, but our own flat. One his parents would live in with us one day. It will be in the city, near our jobs.

Anger surfaced again as she thought about her own parents. How will we be able to look after them in their village?

Lei's imagination took over as she argued with herself. I don't want them to go into a nursing home like some of my older colleagues' parents are doing.

Lei recalled when her class visited nearby nursing homes on a regular basis. The people were cared for and appeared happy but Lei knew they missed their family members who only came to see them during the week of Spring Festival, some not even then. Many of their children were working overseas now and seldom returned to China.

Lei asked herself. How are we going to manage to help care for our parents and pay for Kai's education? She and Yimin had talked about this challenge and agreed that they would both have to earn higher wages. Isn't that why she was back at university?

Lei thought she had Yimin's support to go back for a Master's Degree in Sociology and Political Science. When completed, this degree along with her English degree would guarantee that she could keep her job with the government and proceed up the salary scale. If they could both keep their government jobs they would have housing assistance, medical coverage and retirement pensions. They had decided the government jobs would be the only way they would be able to provide for Kai and both their parents.

Her mind played the devil's advocate reminding her that if she tried to keep this baby they would both lose their government jobs, and be unable to find new ones. They could only be self-employed and there was no future in that at this point in their careers.

Lei started to argue with this dichotomy when Deqeng's face appeared vividly before her. "Give it to us. You know we want a son." The voice was clear and loud.

Her heart pounded quickly, and her breath came in gasps as the muscles in her vagina tightened instinctively to hold the baby safe.

Tears started to flow. She stifled her sobs, aware that the sunrise was filling the bus with radiant light and Deqeng was no longer there.

If only I could turn back the clock, she cried, chewing on her thumb nail.

One of the young girls on the bus coughed in a funny way, as if pointing attention to Lei. The girl flicked her long black hair back around her face and over her shoulder. In the light Lei imagined the girl from Yimin's room. I know it isn't her, she told herself. But then, do I know what or who is real anymore?

She took some deep breaths to stop the heaving in her chest. She can have him, she decided determinedly. Why would I want someone who has betrayed me? She stared at the bruise on her arm where Yimin had held her. She tasted the salty tears on her lips.

Somewhere an owl screeched as she alighted from the bus. Was the owl confirming the end of their love?

*****

Lei lay across her bed on her back. She let herself cry. She had one hand in a fist on her chest where a huge rock seemed to have settled; the opposite hand on her womb where she knew a baby was growing. She already loved it and wanted to protect it. Time was running out. How could she keep this baby when now she knew for sure she didn't have Yimin's support? What was she going to do about his unfaithfulness?

How could he think I could give you away? she spoke with passion to the unborn child. Why hadn't he told me of his plan?

She rolled over on her stomach, feeling the baby protected by her own body. Maybe it isn't his plan. she heard a voice say. Maybe it's only his mother's?

For a moment she wished she could obey her mother-in-law. If Qing became the baby's mother, the children would be cousins as Cezanne explained to her, but in Chinese lineage, they would be called brothers. The same small voice continued, helping her focus on practicalities in spite of herself. Qing would have to go with you to her parents' home on the island of Hainan, as Yimin's mother said.

Could I do it? Could I really give you up? she thought

as her hands slipped between the mattress and her belly. She arched her back, allowing her hands to cradle her womb, as if keeping the baby safe another day.

# CHAPTER 9

After a fitful sleep, Lei decided to skip classes once again and go visit her mother. Surely her mother would understand and support her.

As Lei sat on the bus, she forced thoughts of Yimin out of her mind and reflected on her great love for her mother. She saw her mother and herself in the tall sugarcane rows when she was very young.

"Catch the butterflies," her mother had said, showing her the net she had made for Lei. "Keep them in this jar." At nightfall they would set them free. They always promised each other they would catch them again the next day.

In the early evenings, they would sit around her mother's special chest made of Chinese parasol wood. "This was your grandmother's hair and this was your great grandfather's pigtail," she would say each time they opened the box, dangling the two pieces of hair in front of Lei. "Be careful with them, especially the pigtail. It was a great decision for your grandfather to cut his queue."

Her mother told Lei how in 1912 all Han Chinese men were liberated from shaving their heads and wearing the pig tail. Before this they had been forced to shave the front of their heads and wear the long queue in the Manchu Dynasty. In story-like fashion her mother told Lei how the Han Chinese men did not want to cut their hair as a sign of servitude to the Manchu. The Han Chinese believed from their Confucian teachings that cutting their hair was disrespectful to their ancestors. They believed that everything they owned, even their body with its hair was bestowed upon them by their ancestors. Their filial piety and respect for their ancestors was so strong that they resented this order by the Manchu oppressors, but to disobey would mean death. When the opportunity to stop doing it came in 1912, Lei always imagined her great grandfather treasuring his long hair and wearing it out of respect and gratitude to his ancestors. The ending of the story always fascinated Lei because her mother told her he changed his mind about all these things and he decided to take action and show his independence from tradition and to the fallen Manchu regime. So he chose to cut his pigtail off himself. Some Han Chinese did not have the courage to cut their queues just in case their freedom was short lived, but her great-grandfather survived and passed this independence on to the family.

Recalling this story, Lei recognized she was in a similar position. She had to make a decision like her great-grandfather had done. Suddenly she felt strength from him. If he could break from tradition, then she could too. She would take a stand for other women who were laden down with the burden of duty. But how?

If only he were still alive to help me, she thought. Never mind, he is one with me. He is my ancestor. I hold him in my heart.

The memory box also had faded photographs of her mother and father's wedding day. She remembered asking, "Why are you looking so sad in the picture, Mama?"

"Because I knew once I was married, I wouldn't see my own family again, only at Spring Festival. That would be many months after our wedding."

Two minute silk slippers were the next treasured item in the chest. They were worn by her grandmother and would have confined her to the house. The pain to walk would have been excruciating, but her small feet would have assured a favourable match in marriage. This always fascinated Lei who had loved her independence to run and play as a child.

The chest also held jade jewelry her mother had been given by her family as a dowry. Her mother had never had to sell it, but kept it for security.

Remembering this, Lei thought to ask her mother how much it was worth. Maybe they could sell some to help them pay the fine for a second child.

Little one, what can we do? Lei asked, bringing her attention back to her pregnancy. Your Papa doesn't want you and I don't know what to do. Maybe I will have to give you to Qing. The blood drained from her face. Anxiety set in again as she sat alone on the bus.

She took a deep breath and remembered all her mother had taught her about her inner energy, her chi. Her mother had started teaching her at a young age, and she had insisted Lei accompany her to her Qigong classes.

"Your child is special," she remembered the teacher

saying, as she gently helped her with the many positions, far too many to be remembered by a small child.

"It makes me feel strong and happy," she had told her mother after each session.

"Yes and remembering the proverbs our teacher teaches us, will make you even stronger," her mother had said. Her mind flashed back to a day when her mother read one special one.

"When the map is unrolled, the dagger will be revealed." It seemed to show her that her problems with Gang at school would one day be resolved. Her mother agreed and explained it this way: "It predicts that when the time is right, Gang will be punished in Nature's own way."

Now, years later, Mother and I hold a secret about Gang that even Gang doesn't know we know. I am still waiting for Nature to punish her.

I can't wait, she blurted out silently but with force. I want to punish Gang and Yimin's girlfriend right now. They are my enemies. Resolution in her mind soothed her heart. She sat comforted by the passing scenery. Another proverb her mother had taught her flashed into her mind. 'That the birds of worry and care fly above your head, this you cannot change. But that they build nests in your hair, this you can prevent.'

She got off the bus in YinZhou, the small village where her parents lived. Her father was a doctor at the local hospital and her mother was a nurse at the same hospital.

It was dark when she alighted. Where had the time gone? She felt refreshed by her rest and resolute in her feelings of hatred for Yimin, Gang and the young girl.

Lei made her way carefully along the river embankment to her childhood home. She passed housewives on bicycles, their wheels wobbly from the weight of veggies as well as a chicken or two tied to their handlebars.

She saw peasants lining up at her gate, waiting to ask her father for medicines and herbs. These were people who couldn't afford to see him during the day at the hospital. They knew they wouldn't be turned away if they came to his little office at the entrance to the courtyard.

Her mother was nowhere in sight, so Lei went in and lit a candle on the small table in the living area. She knew the power was off because she had noticed her father working by the light of several candles in his courtyard dispensary.

She closed the sliding glass doors which served as their entrance. She lit another candle and took it with her as she made her way up the steep concrete stairs to her old bedroom. The thermoses of hot water were lined up beside the hand basin in the hallway. She chose one and rinsed her hands and face in the warm well water that her mother had boiled earlier in the day. Feeling exhausted, she decided to go to bed and talk to her mother in the morning. For once a restful sleep enfolded her.

She woke to the crowing of roosters and the barking of dogs. Before going downstairs, she thought about what she was going to say to her mother. Lei felt certain that her mother would help her find a way to keep this baby.

Her mother had always been a progressive thinker. She was influenced by the beliefs of the historic Christian leader Dr. Sun Yat-Sen who led the democratic rebellion in China in 1911. He overthrew the Qing Dynasty and became the first president of the Republic of China. His wife, also called the Mother of China, Soong Ching-Leing, worked for the growing Women's Liberation Organization at that time. She was also a role model for Lei's mother. One of Soong Ching-Leing's first public issues was advocating the ban of arranged marriages. She also initiated the first international magazine about China's reconstruction at that time. She called on other Chinese colleagues like herself and her husband, who had been educated overseas, to write articles to inform foreigners what was happening in China.

"Come and read these magazines," her mother would say, proudly displaying the recent editions of the magazine, China Today. They were not banned, but were still scrutinized carefully by the censors for anti-communist thought.

Lately her mother had been reading her Bible and attending a house church in the neighbourhood.

"Be careful, Mama. The government has issued warnings that house churches are illegal and any gathering of people must be registered," Lei had cautioned.

"I am intrigued Lei, by what part of Christianity must have influenced Dr. Sun Yat-Sen. Did you know he was a Christian?" she asked and continued, not waiting for an answer, "When he went to study in Hawaii he became a Christian. I think that is why he wanted a social revolution for his people. He wanted all the groups in China to unite: the Han, Mongols, Tibetans, Manchus and Muslims. He argued, as the Bible also does, that we share a common blood, it doesn't matter if our skin is a different colour or we speak a different language. He wanted democracy for China. She remembered her mother telling her that Soong Ching-Leing quoted a line from Abraham Lincoln's Gettysburg Address, 'government of the people, by the people, for the people'. Did you know that Lei?"

Lei hadn't heard this phrase before, but it stayed in her heart. It affected how she related to foreigners; she was open to their friendship, whereas her colleagues were suspicious of them. She had tried to talk to her father about the similarity of Lincoln's ideals with Communist ideology, but he always avoided her attempts to engage him in discussion.

Hearing a noise downstairs, Lei called out, "You there Mama?'

Getting no answer, she headed for the kitchen. She found only her father already eating his steamed rice and snake beans.

"Come and sit down." He pointed his chopsticks at the rice pot for her to help herself.

"Where's Mama?"

"She's gone to take one of my elderly patients to the

hospital in Ningbo."

"Oh," disappointment was sharp in her voice.

Her father continued to eat, slurping his rice as he tilted his bowl to his mouth. With a final loud slurp he emptied it.

"Why did you come at this time of the week?"

"I want to talk to Mama about something important."

He must have noticed her eyes were puffy and red from crying and she was not her usual self. She started to tell him about her situation, unconsciously hoping she could change his attitude about the One Child Policy if he realized how it was affecting his only daughter.

"I want another child."

"Forget it, you know the law and you're intelligent enough to know it is best for our motherland. Be thankful you have a son; wait for a grandson. You are getting a housing allowance and Kai is getting special gifts from the government because you and Yimin are obeying the law. Do you want those benefits to stop?" Her father took a breath as if considering what else to say. Before Lei had time to respond, he continued, "Do you want a black baby? You know that a black baby can never get an ID number to go to a government school or work at a government job in China. These children must be sent overseas for education or work in private businesses or worse still end up in slavery or prostitution."

She knew from the way her father spoke, it was impossible to communicate further. It's always this way, she thought. Her love for her father made her listen patiently while he told her all the reasons the government saw fit to enforce this policy.

He reminded her of the family that had their house bulldozed because they couldn't pay the fine for a second child. "And they took their bikes away, remember? How could they get to work?"

While he was speaking, she thought, "He's really covering up his fear for my freedom as a woman in China. Why can't he say that?"

Her father had suffered during the Cultural Revolution because of his family background. He was forced to confess to the Party that his father had been a counter-revolutionary. Her grandfather had been labeled an Ox Demon and a Snake Spirit, opposing Mao's thought. Although this was all in the past, Lei knew he still felt this stigma of his ancestors. Her father had been forced to join the Communist Army and he had become a 'barefoot' doctor, learning all he knew in the battle field. He now towed a strict party line insisting that Lei and her mother follow all Party policies. Many of her mother's more insightful beliefs were shared only with Lei for fear of upsetting her father.

Her father's voice interrupted her thoughts.

"It's now a law Lei, not just a policy. It changed in 2003. You must obey it."

Lei decided not to tell her father it was already too late. She was sure he wouldn't understand her 'mistake', nor Yimin's infidelity either.

She took a deep breath to calm herself. I don't want him to lose respect for Yimin. It's okay for me to hate Yimin, but not my father, at least not yet. She shuddered, in fear that she had spoken her thought out loud.

"I'd better go," she said, her voice calm and loving again.

They walked side by side back through the village. Lei headed out to the bus stop and her father made his way to the hospital. Lei realized how much she loved him. He was a good man and followed what he thought was right. He had overcome his background and studied hard to become a real doctor. He had fallen in love with her mother while he was an intern at her hospital.

On the bus Lei continued to contemplate her father's medical career. She wondered if Chinese doctors had to swear an oath to preserve life. Her mother told her western doctors have to do this. If they did, she wondered how her father would reconcile this oath with the forced abortions required to implement the One Child Policy.

The more Lei thought about this, the madder she got. Surely her father knew what happened to the millions of unborn babies in China. He must see the waste bins full of dead infants at his own hospital, and hear the cries of their mothers?

Why could she not argue with him, reason with him. She wanted to tell him about her colleague who was dragged to the hospital and her baby injected with a saline solution that was meant to kill it and bring on a natural abortion. When it didn't work, she had told Lei how they had cut up the baby with scissors, so they could take out pieces of it one at a time. The image of a tiny foot with five little toes being held on the end of the nurse's tongs would haunt her friend forever.

Is this what my father would want for me if he found out I was pregnant?

Lei rode home in panic. She was suddenly aware of the full consequences of her decision.

## CHAPTER 10

Her mother arrived at the dormitory early the next morning. Lei had known that she would come.

Her mother was thirty-nine when students demonstrated for political change in Beijing's Tianamnen Square. Lei was nineteen.

"I am too old to go to Beijing, Lei, but I do want to talk about it with you." She recalled her mother saying.

Lei had realized then how politically active her mother must have been in her youth. It was one of the family stories how in 1978, the year Lei was eight, her mother took her with her as she made a pilgrimage to Beijing's Democracy Wall. The wall had been erected by the government to honour freedom of speech. Her mother went specifically to read the famous essay by Wei

Jingsheng, the Chinese intellectual who was the best known Chinese human rights and democracy advocate at that time. Her mother often reminded Lei that his essay said the economic reform program in China was useless unless the people were given democracy in every sense of the word. He criticized the government by calling them "shameless bandits," no better than capitalists who robbed workers of their money earned by their sweat and blood.

Wei Jingsheng was considered by the international community at the University to be the Chinese Mandela. Wei had fought for human rights without regard for the cost to himself. He had spent a total of eighteen years in Chinese jails before being exiled to the United States. The sad part was that two months after the Democratic Wall was put up it had been removed and a regulation passed prohibiting any material opposed to the government. Those who had posted slogans, poetry or essays were rounded up and sent for rehabilitation in work camps. Lei's mother mourned Jingsheng's imprisonment but had been unable to speak openly about it.

*****

Lei had the afternoon full of classes so her mother rested in her room till she returned. Lei had a hard time concentrating on her lectures. Her mind kept wandering back to her time with her father. She wondered if he had guessed her condition, or had just repeated their conversation to her mother who had then put two and two together? Her mother had arrived with a bag of dried ginger and chamomile flowers to make tea. This infusion of ingredients was renowned for easing a woman's first stages of morning sickness. Likely she already knew Lei's secret. She thought suddenly of another saying: "A secret is like a dove, when it leaves my hand it takes wing."

When Lei returned from her morning classes, she found her mother cooking some fresh rice in Lei's electric cooker and steaming green vegetables on top of the rice. When they had cooked, they sat on the bed, their hands wrapped around their warm bowls of rice and veggies.

"When did it happen?"

"Just two weeks ago," replied Lei, thinking of Yimin's infidelity.

"How can that be?"

Realizing her mistake, Lei told her what had happened with Yimin, adding at the end that she was pregnant again.

"Being pregnant, Lei, is a wonderful blessing, but Yimin's behaviour is unacceptable."

"He wants me to have another abortion and I won't have one."

"Of course you won't." Her mother's eyebrows were lowered, a frown of disapproval. She hadn't known about Lei's first abortion. At that time Lei had thought she was doing what was right and hadn't wanted to involve her own family. Only Yimin's family knew and of course they were silent once they knew of her automatic decision to follow the law.

"I'm sorry I never told you, Mama. I've already had one abortion. It was my fault I got pregnant and I had to take care of it. This time it's my fault again, but I want to keep it."

"Of course. We will find a way to keep this cherished one," she said as she stood and hugged her daughter, her right hand stroking Lei's belly.

"Precious treasure worth cherishing." Lei remembered the proverb her mother had taught her so long ago. It gave her hope. They sat again in silence, strong in their united decision to find a way to keep the baby.

Lei knew her mother had wanted a second child after

she was born, but before she could conceive again the Government brought in the One Child Policy. Her father embraced the law immediately. He judged harshly any peasant or citizen who disobeyed the new recipe for China's economic recovery and growth, but China did not have the natural resources to support the staggering population growth that Chairman Mao had foolishly demanded. "Bear as many children as possible," he had said, "to make China stronger." Now the government was saying, "Less babies, more prosperity." The One Child Policy was seen as the solution.

Lei remembered one night when she was about eight, her mother and father were having a heated argument. She snuck down the stairs and hid on the first landing and listened.

"She needs a brother to protect her."

"My brother's sons will protect her."

"They're not real brothers," she heard her mother sob. Her father's back was turned to her mother.

"Your parents are willing to pay the money to the Family Planning Committee if we will give them a grandson."

"And how can you be sure of that?"

Only now did Lei understand the sarcasm in his voice.

"Are you willing to have an abortion or get rid of it if it's another girl?"

Lei hadn't known what the word abortion meant, but it was a word she had chosen to remember. Her father's voice was angry.

Sitting crouched up on the landing, out of sight, she tried to make sense of her parents' angry words. She never doubted her mother's love and although her father was aloof, like most Chinese fathers, she assumed he felt the same as her mother. He proudly displayed their One Child Family Certificate they received each year for following the law. But this was something different. Suddenly, Lei realized her father had wished she had been born a boy.

She had never thought about it before, but now Lei wondered. Was my mother pregnant the night they argued? Or was she just testing my father's willingness to let his parents pay the "social alimony," if she did get pregnant again?

"Were you already pregnant, Mama?"

"Yes, and I did what was necessary at that time. Today I would try to keep it." Tears filled her eyes as she looked earnestly at Lei.

Lei's imagination ran wild. How had she got rid of it? Had she had an abortion or drowned it at birth or given it away? Was there a brother somewhere to help them?

Lei couldn't bring herself to ask her mother. She wanted to solve her own problem. They sat in silence for some time.

"Has Gang visited you yet?" her mother asked, breaking into her thoughts.

"No, she doesn't know."

"Well then, leave and have the baby in secret. I will help you." Her mother continued to cradle her as they sat on the bed.

"But Yimin doesn't want it. He wants me to give it to Dageng and Qing," she found herself saying. Tears started to stream down her face and her shoulders shook with her sobs.

"Do you think you could do this?" her mother said as she stroked her hair.

"No, I want this baby for Kai and myself. I've even been thinking that maybe I could go and study overseas and have it born in Canada or America, so it would have foreign citizenship. Or even Hong Kong. Aren't they secretly allowing women to go there to have a baby and get their birth papers there?

"Think carefully about such a decision, Lei, you would have to leave Kai behind and I am afraid Yimin's family would never let you have him again. I think you would have to have a pregnancy test before you leave the country too. I recently heard of a professor from the University of Beijing having her second child in London where she was a student, and now she is being sent back to China. The only solution she has is to divorce her husband who is also a professor at the same university. If they get a divorce and she goes to live somewhere else in China with the second child, her husband will not be punished for their disobeying the law. But she will be heartbroken because she truly loves her husband. She is under a lot of pressure because the head of the university is being punished for allowing one of his staff to disobey the law.

Silence filled the room while they both reflected on this scenario.

"What if we all contribute to the fine and let you have the baby here with us?" her mother said with a smile on her face.

"But what about Yimin? I told you, he's having an affair. I caught him at his factory dorm with a young girl. They were drinking together and she was in bed with him." Lei choked as she got to the end of the sentence realizing she'd blocked out this picture for the past days. The pain of it surrounded her heart and she felt like it would shrivel to nothing. She turned and buried her head in her mother's shoulder.

Her mother massaged her back and shoulders. Her soothing voice told her to let Yimin go. "You can divorce him and still have the baby in secret. You can go to my sister in the countryside. We will all help you. She can look after the baby for you. You can take Kai and have the baby too. I'm sure Yimin would agree to this."

Lei hadn't heard all her mother said. She was allowing herself to think for the first time of the word divorce. It had never entered her consciousness as a possibility.

Her mother continued, "Haven't you heard, in China now they say on TV, the national greeting is not 'Have you eaten?' but 'Have you divorced?' Even big companies are advertising for divorced people because they don't have to support a whole family. Some people are divorcing just so they can get a job."

Lei had not known this and the idea was frightening. Could she live without Yimin? Suddenly she felt compelled to find him and to tell him that she wanted a divorce. What would he say? But could she have the baby alone? Would Yimin let her still keep Kai? What about her job? Would they find out about her baby?

Lei's mother continued to talk about where she could go to have the baby. She was adamant that divorce was the answer to the 'other woman'. She stressed that she would support her daughter.

Lei couldn't help feeling that this was what her mother must have wished for herself years ago. Suddenly she too missed the brother she had never had. He wouldn't have been like Yimin or even her father, she was sure of it. She was sure he'd have been there for her mother and herself. He would have protected them. He might even have driven Gang away.

Her mother glanced at her watch, indicating she should leave. Lei rose from the bed as her mother prepared for her return to the village. She could tell that her mother thought that they had agreed on a plan.

"You must leave for the countryside soon, before Gang discovers your pregnancy. She's been bragging about what an efficient job she's doing for the government. We all know she means for her father, not the government. No one trusts her father or her. She visited us recently and asked how you were. Maybe she suspects you are pregnant. Some Buddhist women tried to scare her by telling her evil things would happen to her if she keeps taking babies from women's wombs. She didn't believe them of course and reported the old women to the police. I heard she is also selling the dead fetuses for medicine made to help impotent men and to make beauty products for women. You must leave soon before she discovers that you are pregnant."

"Wait Mama. How can I get a divorce, and how will I stop the baby from being a black baby? How can I take Kai with me? Yimin's parents will never let me take him."

"I will find out the details for a divorce. As for an ID number for the baby, I know someone through the hospital who can sell us an ID number." She took a breath before continuing.

"I will tell your in-laws we are going to take Kai to visit our family in the countryside. They will know what we are doing, but I am sure that they won't interfere or they will lose face. Maybe you can even tell them you plan to give it to Qing and Dageng. You could agree and then change your mind after it's born."

"That would be so terrible for Qing, Mama. I don't think I could do that to her."

"Well, think about what you can do Lei, you must think of yourself, not Qing. You must make a decision soon and stick to it."

"What about my studies?"

"Forget them until you come back. You'll be a divorced woman by then and maybe you can take your children and go overseas to study."

Lei's mother promised to contact her as soon as she found out the requirements for divorce. She would contact her sister in the neighbouring province to see if they could stay with her family. Her mother was confident that they had a plan, but could she make it her own?

They parted, their clasped hands lingering, neither woman wanting to let go.

# CHAPTER 11

Wang's dormitory room was across the hallway from Yimin's. Returning home from his late shift at the factory, Wang had passed Lei as she struggled down the darkened hallway on the fateful evening she discovered Yimin with his lover. Earlier in the evening Wang had been at the nightclub when Yimin had left with the young girl. Entering their hallway on the second floor, he had heard the loud crash of the broken mirror. Yimin's doorway was open and he saw him slumped on his bed with his head in his hands.

Wang had glanced at the fragments of the broken bottle, and made a decision. He knew he could leave and let Yimin sort out his own problems or he could do as The Big Book said, and offer his support.

"Want to talk about it?" Wang said, entering the room.

Keeping his head down, Yimin shook it, muttering, "No, it's too late. I've lost her."

"That's what you think Yimin, but it doesn't always work that way."

Yimin ignored Wang and staggered to the toilet where he vomited repeatedly.

Wang made them both a cup of coffee from the hot water in the thermos.

"I shouldn't have gone to the club tonight," Yimin lamented, dropping himself in the chair beside Wang.

"It's not too late Yimin, you can stop this heavy drinking and take control of your life. Right now the alcohol is controlling you."

"It's not the alcohol, it's that girl. She is sex crazy."

"And so are you when you're drinking. Stop the drinking and you won't have these feelings for anyone else but your wife."

"But I need another drink. Do you have anything?"

"Yimin, leave it alone while we talk. I'll make you another coffee. You said you didn't want to lose Lei and I promise you, if you stop drinking you will keep her. There is Kai to think about too. You don't want to lose him either."

"You're right, but I don't think I drink too much," Yimin argued, his voice defensive.

"Do you remember inviting the girl back to your apartment?"

"No, the last thing I remember was buying a round of drinks for everyone. She was with the mother-in-law gang that protects our factory. She must have brought me here when I passed out."

"Think about it Yimin, you can't even remember the details. Do you want to lose Lei and Kai just for some gang girl?"

Yimin was having trouble staying awake, but Wang wanted to keep him talking. He poured him another coffee.

Yimin spoke up as if he knew Wang was trying to help. "I never do anything right. Just ask my father, he'll tell you. They should have sent Dageng to university, not me. I wish he could have gotten the grades I got in school."

Wang listened patiently, knowing that listening was better than talking right now.

"But I'm going to make it up to my family. I'm going to get rich and look after everyone. Then father will be happy, but Lei won't be because I'm going to make her give our baby to my brother. Maybe then he will forgive me for failing everyone."

"You never told me Lei was expecting again Yimin. That is serious. We will all be punished. Why hasn't she had an abortion?"

"She won't and I can't make her. She wants to keep it. I told her about everyone losing their bonuses but she won't listen. And we can't afford a second child. She must give it to Qing."

"Have you told her this, Yimin?"

"No, but my mother has. It was her idea."

"Have another cup of coffee, Yimin. I'll go warm up some dumplings for us."

When Wang returned from his room with the dumplings on a plate, he found Yimin sprawled across the bed, face down. He was asleep.

Wang adjusted Yimin to a better angle so he could lie beside him. He wanted to be there when Yimin woke.

Hours passed and dawn shone through the thin curtains.

"Why are you here?" Yimin asked Wang as he fumbled his way to the toilet. The sound of his vomiting filled the room.

"I wanted to talk with you about last night."

"It's too late, I've lost Lei. She'll never understand."

"You mean about the girl or about your drinking or the pregnancy?"

"All of it. If I hadn't been drinking, the girl wouldn't have been here."

"Why were you drinking?"

"I don't know. It just happens. I used to be able to drink with everyone but now I get drunk so fast." He attempted to smooth his rumpled hair.

"And I have to drink. My bosses want me to entertain the bosses of our factory protectors or we will lose all our equipment and shipments. He says when they are with me at night, they aren't on our property seeing what is happening or vandalizing our factory. You know we have so many prisoners from the local laogai. They are doing their reform through labour at our factory, but our bosses do not want their competition factories to know just how many men we have. It's their labour that's our profit."

"That's crazy Yimin. You can't live like this."

"I have to, it's my job."

"Come with me Yimin, to a meeting where you will learn some tools to take back your life. I promise you, with this program you will be able to win Lei back and manage your life again."

"What meeting are you talking about?" Yimin stretched, releasing the tension in his back. He wanted to go back to sleep.

"Don't fall asleep Yimin. I want you to commit to coming to just one meeting of the Alcoholics Anonymous group. I swear you will find the strength to give up all this drinking and start to live a life blessed by the gods."

"Would you come with me, Wang?"

"Yes, of course. I'll come back today after my shift so you won't be alone. The meeting is tomorrow night at 8:00 o'clock in the outpatients' coffee room of the Shanghai hospital. I'll pick you up at 4:00 o'clock. We should make it. You'll be back in time to do the graveyard shift."

\*\*\*\*\*

Wang and Yimin sat in the meeting room. Though the AA organization had been sanctioned in China in 1999, a hospital staff member was required to be present.

Yimin sat quietly in the circle of men, all of them, except for Wang, strangers. He listened to their stories but found his mind drifting back to the previous night when Wang had returned as promised.

Wang had sat long into the night with Yimin. Wang had listened while he talked about his relationship with Lei. Yimin had been willing to admit he was wrong. He was a father and a husband. He knew he shouldn't have been with another woman, even though it was a common practice in China. Wang had sidestepped this issue and instead led him down a path of discovery about his drinking.

When did it start? Was his father or mother a drinker? How long could he go without a drink? Yimin was honest with his answers and admitted he drank almost daily now. He said it started once Lei had restricted their lovemaking according to a rhythm method she was using after Kai was born. On her 'off days' he would pour himself a drink before he went to sleep. He'd heat it up country style and tell himself it was just to help him sleep. He also had to drink most evenings with the gang that protected the factory. He liked to play the table game of matching hand signals with each other, the winner having to drink their full glass of beer in one go. Many times he had come back to the dormitory totally drunk.

Yimin didn't think his parents were heavy drinkers but he knew his grandfather made his own rice wine with rainwater. He admitted they all liked to drink it when they got together.

When Wang had asked about Lei, he remembered responding, "She's always studying now and too tired to have sex. I know I'm attracted to other women, but it's only when I'm drunk. This was the first time I ever brought a woman to my dormitory with me. I don't even remember asking her. I think she brought me home in her car."

"How would she get by the guard at the gate?" Wang asked.

"I don't know. I probably asked them to let us in." He added with desperation in his voice, "Wang, please help me. I don't want to lose Lei."

"Yimin, trust the program. Even our government recognizes many of our people need this program. They are allowing groups to meet in different hospitals throughout the country. Just take step one and trust your Higher Power," Wang had said calmly.

"But I've always relied on myself. I can't trust a god I don't even know. And now you are saying Higher

Power. What do you mean?"

Wang ignored his question and asked if it was working.

"Is what working? Yimin asked.

"Relying on yourself all the time?"

Yimin had left the question unanswered. At the meeting, Yimin had said very little. Other members of the group spoke up, each addressing their own situation. No one criticized another. This was rare in Chinese society. Self criticism was still taught in schools.

As Yimin listened, he began to hear familiar stories. He was not alone in his unfaithfulness. Many had lost their jobs, their wives and families. Many had gained them back only to lose them again as they went down "slippery slopes" as they called it when they started to drink again.

Wang did his best to convince Yimin that he had a disease that led him to drink too much; that he was allergic to alcohol. The attending medical staff supported this belief with research that had been done in the West. Wang went on with the assurance that once he gave up alcohol, other things in his life would come out right. To Yimin, that meant that Lei wouldn't leave him. In his heart he saw a ray of hope illuminating a path before him.

\*\*\*\*\*

Yimin didn't go to Lei's dormitory on the following night; he wanted to be sure that what he was doing was really going to work. He had taken the first step and admitted he was helpless over alcohol and his life had become unmanageable. This was a mind decision and his heart was facing up to his responsibility for Lei's pregnancy. He could have had a vasectomy or used condoms rather than relying on Lei to use the pill after her abortion. He sat in his factory office reading The Little Red Book that Wang had lent him. It was a translated copy of the Big Red Book written by two westerners who had saved each other from a life of alcoholism.

Was the program really going to be enough to sort out the mess he was in? Yimin searched for the answers.

Hours later when Wang walked by his office window, he called out, "What did you say I had to do?"

"Just come to the meetings. There's one every night and sometimes at lunch time. Use the phone list of members they gave you if you feel yourself slipping back into dangerous behaviour or depressed thoughts. We'll always be there to help. Every one of us has been in your shoes.

Remember the confidentiality though and don't share what you heard at the meeting with non AA members."

Warmth radiated from Wang. Yimin had never experienced such a feeling from another Chinese man.

His mind was full of questions. Does Wang know what he is saying? Could this program work? Can I just drink cola with the gang at the night clubs? Maybe I should stop going to the clubs? What about Lei and the baby? Can I really promise to help her keep this baby? How will I tell my mother?

# CHAPTER 12

Ian's cell phone rang. He was in front of his computer. He looked cautiously over his shoulder when he saw the call was an international one. Alone in his Bond street apartment, twenty-three floors up with an uninterrupted view of the famous Pearl Tower of Shanghai, he knew he was unobserved. The glance was unnecessary, but the code they would use was a realistic measure against the government hackers who might be intercepting the call.

"21:00 hours, ninth of the tenth," he heard.

"Wrong number," he said in Mandarin, pressing the end key.

He turned to his computer and logged onto the scheduled plan, again in code. He entered the numbers he had been given, and e-mailed them out to his waiting company. He logged off and stuffed his Qigong clothes into his sports bag. He headed to the Crowne Plaza gymnasium. He felt himself relaxing into his role of student. He had only to place himself in his Teacher's hands, absorbing all he could of the ancient philosophy and technique of cultivating one's life force.

In the back of his mind he was toying with the very real possibility that his e-mails were being intercepted.

# CHAPTER 13

Gang moved with heavy effort. Her hip defect, left untreated at birth, gave her constant pain. She knew it was no secret that it was only because she was the daughter of a party cadre that she had been allowed to live and make her own way in the world. She had witnessed babies with this same defect drowned or abandoned by their frightened and disappointed mothers. Her father had told her it was only because her mother insisted he let her live that he relented and did not send her away immediately. She knew he resented her. Gang envied girls like Lei who had perfect hips and long straight legs.

She never wished she was dead but rather that the

perfect ones were dead. When Gang's mother discovered her nasty nature, she gave up her nurturing and passed her to a poor village woman to rear through primary school. When Middle School days started, her father allowed her to return home. Her mother had missed her and wanted them to give her another chance. But it was too late. The damage to Gang's psyche was permanent. She was determined to maim others so she could gloat over their imperfections. She was the only perfect one in her exercise of power.

Could her whole development have changed course when she found a friend in Bai? Bai had loved her unconditionally. He saw her whole before he even did the operation he promised to perform to correct her hips. She had blossomed with his love. She hadn't shared this nasty side of her personality. There seemed no need when he was in her life. His parents' total rejection of her brought her back to reality.

Her father also had a corrupt plan for her. After Gang failed to get into university, he used his influence in the party to get her appointed as the Head of the Family Planning Committee in Cixi, where he was Chief of Public Works. Her father initiated her into fraudulent dealings, showing her ways she could become rich, even without the support of a husband.

Gang not only collected her basic salary from the Central Government, but she managed to collect double or more in excess of her salary by her own ingenious schemes for people who couldn't pay the fine for a second child. Most of this money had to be turned over to her father who then parceled out small amounts to her at his discretion. But there were still some dealings he didn't know about.

"Let's go and find Lei," Gang said to her two co-workers. "I know she was visiting her father yesterday. I have proof she is pregnant again."

The early morning dew cleansed the air, masking the fumes from the coal burners where breakfast congee simmered. Vendors sold fresh rollups. They took orders from the cluster of office-bound workers waiting to tell them if they wanted one egg or two and whether they would have strips of fried wheat in the tortilla-like roll.

The eyes of the customers left the cooks and watched the determined Neighbourhood Committee follow Gang as she lurched intently onwards with her uneven gait.

# CHAPTER 14

Lei's father had not gone to work yet. He sat with Lei at the small folding table on low plastic stools in their sitting room. The savoury aroma of small rice cakes with coriander leaves heating in the heavy wok made the pained silence around the table bearable.

"Where is Yimin?" her father asked.

Lei had decided to tell him of Yimin's unfaithfulness. They were interrupted by the two yard dogs barking, announcing the presence of the women crossing the courtyard. They had unlatched the gate and let themselves in. The hair on the dogs' necks and backs stood up as they bared their teeth. In spite of Gang's limp, she was agile enough to bend down to get a stone to throw and at the same time shout abuse at the dogs. Their courage waned and they slunk back, continuing to growl deep in their throats.

Gang shouted through the doorway, "Come with us, Lei. You have to have a medical test."

"What are you talking about?" Lei responded, defiance in her voice. She did her best to hide the panicky feeling in her stomach.

"We know you're pregnant. And you're going to get rid of it."

"Do what they say." She heard her father's firm voice, as he stood and tried to assist her to stand up and join them.

How could he agree? Lei felt strangely dissociated in spite of her danger. What made a party policy more important than the desire of his only daughter? Couldn't he see that this law of forced abortions was an archaic law? That it was no longer serving to solve the population problem but rather lining the pockets of the Neighbourhood Committee members? Could he not see that forced abortions were just legal genocide of unwanted babies?

She had no time to question her father's thinking as they pushed him aside and seized her shoulders, forcing her arms behind her. Her foot tangled in the legs of the plastic stool as she attempted to rise and pull away. Just as she tried to jerk herself free, her mother appeared from the kitchen. A kettle of steaming water was in her hand.

"Let her go," she said. "This is boiling, and you'll be getting it in the face if you don't let her go." Her other hand wielded a huge chopping knife.

The eyes of her captors grew large as they realized her mother's intent. They released Lei and backed away. Lei had just enough time to run across the courtyard through the open gate to the alleyway.

She ran along the narrow laneways, following the riverbank to the open space, hoping for a crowded bus to conceal herself. Finding one, she realized she had no purse. Fighting down her panic she begged the driver to let her ride this once without paying. He agreed.

Lei refused to let the welling tears overflow. Adrenalin ran through her veins. She knew her face was flushed from her escape. She tried to sit up straight and questioned, "Which is stronger, my hatred for Gang and her committee or my anger at my father?" She daren't think that it might have been him who informed them of her pregnancy.

Her wrists still pained her where the women had held her. She massaged them. She would not let herself give in to despair. Lei was more determined than ever to keep this baby, but how?

# CHAPTER 15

"I must see you." Lei spoke into her dormitory phone.

It was clear now that she must divorce Yimin and find a way to keep this baby herself. She had decided she wouldn't give it to Qing. She would follow her mother's plan.

"Okay," said Yimin. "I'll meet you tonight after work in the Flower Garden Park." There was softness in his voice she hadn't heard before.

The park was brightly lit with lanterns and burning joss sticks in front of the Daoist shrine. Lovers held hands on benches and strolled together on the footpath. Times had changed. Couples needed to be introduced and also continually chaperoned until marriage. Underneath this veneer of propriety, many marriages in the past were the result of young female Red Guards being forced to sleep with the officers of the People's Liberation Army as their "duty" to their country; their innocence and virginity being lost as early as twelve and thirteen years old. Oblivious of the irony of its reversals, the law now decreed that a woman could not marry until age twenty-two. To keep a job in many big firms, female workers were routinely checked to ensure that their virginity was still intact. Pregnancy tests were mandatory by most firms. Refusing them meant no job interview. Once hired, monthly checks were expected and birth control forms had to be filled out yearly to show that individuals were conforming.

Lei spotted Yimin's slim silhouette as he stood by the lotus blossom lake. He was crushing out one cigarette and lighting another.

Lei's breath was short, her posture stooped. Could she go through with this confrontation? She knew her baby was already developing. She was sure she saw a swelling of her belly when she was in the shower. Her breasts were changing too.

She stepped forward before she had time to weaken. The scene of the girl in Yimin's room flashed before her.

She knew she would demand a divorce.

"Where have you been?" he asked gently. "I've been trying to find you all night. Where is your phone?"

"I left it at my mother's house this afternoon. I had an appointment after class with my professor."

At that instant, Yimin's phone rang. He handed it to Lei when he heard her mother's voice.

"They've taken your purse," her mother said frantically. "Gang is determined to have her way. She showed us your ID card. She says she will meet you at our house tomorrow night if you want it back. Be sure to come Lei, I am afraid they will hurt your father."

Lei hung up, obviously agitated from the information her mother had given her. What would Gang do to her family? She knew Gang had the power to put her father in jail, for no other reason than she wanted to. They could keep him there till she agreed to have an abortion. How could she do that to her parents?

Pushing her fears out of her mind, she decided to deal with Yimin first.

"I want a divorce."

"What? Lei, what are you talking about? Surely you don't think that is the answer to our problems? You know I love you."

"But the other girl?"

"Lei, I'm so sorry. It's the first time I've ever done anything like that and I don't even remember taking her to my room. Please forgive me. I know it's my drinking that I must stop and I promise I will. I have a plan."

He gathered her in his arms and although she had resolved to hate him, her heart melted as she allowed her head to rest on his chest. It felt like the life within her stirred. A hope awoke in her that together they could fight Gang.

"What about the baby?" she asked as he gently kissed her forehead, brushing her damp hair aside.

"If you want to keep it Lei, I promise to help you find a way."

Lei looked at him. Hope stirred. Could he really mean it?

"I thought you wanted me to give the baby to Dageng and Qing?"

"That was my mother's idea. I knew it would be a great sacrifice for you, but mother thought it would allow you to keep the baby, and we could see it whenever we wanted. Think about it Lei, it is one of the solutions."

Lei sighed, overwhelmed by her situation and options.

"Mother just told me Gang wants to meet me tomorrow night at their house. If I don't go I know she will punish them."

The silence was overwhelming as they felt the futility of their situation. Lei questioned her heart. Why couldn't Gang forget the past. Why couldn't she be on their side, and turn her head as some Neighbourhood Committee heads did? Would Gang leave them alone if Lei told her that Gang's child was still alive, and not dead like she was told?

Yimin broke her thoughts, suddenly brightening and said "Let's go to my Aunty in the monastery just outside of town. She is there on a retreat. She will help us decide the best plan."

Heading for the bus station together, Lei allowed Yimin to hold her hand. Her heart softened. She knew she wanted to trust him. Their eyes met and he squeezed her hand in reassurance. As they walked, he told her about his AA meetings.

It seemed he believed he had some kind of illness. The illness could only be cured if he stopped drinking.

Lei could only ask, "Are you sure?" when he finished explaining about it. He did his best to reassure her but felt his own fears at the same time. He wanted to phone Wang and let him talk to her but he didn't want to confuse her with all the strategies Wang said he must use to overcome his need for a drink.

They eventually arrived at Aunty Mei's small cubicle. They passed miniature Buddhist shrines in the hallway outside her doorway.

Aunt Mei listened to their story calmly, but could not hide her agitation when she heard of Gang's demand.

"We have visited with many girls like you, Lei. Often we are too late. Gang had forced them to have abortions; some ran away halfway through the procedure and bled to death. Others paid her for medicine she promised would abort the babies. When it didn't, they hid themselves thinking all would be well, but they gave birth to deformed or handicapped babies. Others committed suicide. Gang is ruthless Lei, she will try to destroy your life."

Yimin's Aunty took Lei's hands in hers. "We have told her these dead babies will come one day to do her harm. All the corrupt money and praise from the Central

Government for her efficiency will be nothing. She will one day understand that a human being begins at the instant of conception when sperm, egg and *vijñāna* come together."

Still holding Lei's hands, Aunt Mei looked directly at Yimin and Lei. "You and your families will also be harmed if you destroy this life. Lei, I am sure it is the spirit of the baby you already aborted who wants to come again to your womb."

She stood, releasing their hands. "The first thing we must do is go to the Jizo altar and recite the Jizo dharn for the benefit of the unborn child. You know Jizo is the Bodhisattva of the earth womb. He is a child monk who carries the bright jewel of Dharm Truth whose Light banishes all fear. This deity will protect you and your unborn baby and give you the courage you need, Lei. He will also protect your families."

Aunty Mei left to purchase the necessary joss sticks to burn at the altar. When she returned, two monks moving like ministering angels helped her prepare the altar.

Aunty Mei asked them again if they were committed to protecting this unborn child. Yimin immediately said, "Yes." Lei sensed a strengthening of his character. He must know that this decision would endanger his job, his relationship with his family and their financial security.

Lei needed no encouragement to say yes to Aunt Mei. She agreed that if Jizo was the protector of children born and unborn, then perhaps as Aunty said, the life within her was the same child she had aborted earlier, this time a bit more conscious and determined to have entry into this time and space. Lei no longer doubted that she was going to save the baby.

"You must leave your studies and Yimin his job and come live with me," she said to Lei. "Guizhou is far enough away from Zhejiang that they won't follow you. You can bring Kai and I will mind him while you work in our small shop. Yimin can go to work with my son. The plum orchards are needing pickers. If my Neighbourhood Committee asks questions we can say this is your first child and that Kai is my sister's child. After all, we are Miao and we can have as many children as we like. I know someone who can get us an ID card made for this precious baby. My family will help you and I know your mother will too. Don't worry about your father Lei, he can take care of himself."

*****

In her room that night, Lei lay in Yimin's arms. Suddenly Lei heard herself giving voice to her thoughts. "Are you sure you don't want to see that girl again?"

"Never," he said quickly, "and I will never drink again. I'm allergic to the stuff. This move to Guizhou will be good for us. We can start fresh."

"But what about your brother?"

"Maybe we still should consider letting Qing have the baby."

Lei's look of shock made him instantly add, "After it's grown a bit. They could come to visit and if they were still keen and you were willing, they could move to Guizhou too. We could start that technical pig farm I studied about at university. You might even be able to continue your studies online like Cezanne does."

"You must be crazy," she said. "Didn't you hear what Aunty said? This baby is meant to be with us. I know it in my heart."

Yimin was silent. She wrapped her arms around her raised knees raised as if to protect the baby she was carrying. "How could I give you up," she silently murmured. "Was that still an option? Can I truly trust Yimin? Will he be strong enough to stand up to his own mother?"

Yimin shifted in the bed. He curled himself around Lei, his hands searching out her breasts. He didn't try to arouse her.

# CHAPTER 16

Lei called her mother first thing in the morning. "I don't need a divorce, Mama. Yimin has promised it will never happen again. He says it's because he has been drinking too much. He promised me he is going to stop drinking. 'Cold turkey' he called it."

"Can you believe him?"

"Mama, I want to. He is a good man. He's never done anything like this before."

"Be careful, Lei. Take your time. Don't forget to come this afternoon. Gang is planning to meet us here. She said not to tell anyone. She said she has a deal for you."

"Do you believe her, Mama? Why did you agree to meet her?"

"Your father said we'd better. She has a lot of power,

Lei. She could ruin everyone in this family, and Yimin's family too."

"Okay, we'll be there."

Lei closed her phone. Could they really make a deal with Gang? What had her mother done that made Gang even consider helping them? Had her mother threatened Gang with information about Gang's own illegitimate child who somehow had escaped being sold for begging in the cities? Was it Gang's mother who was protecting the child? Why didn't Gang's mother tell her what had happened to her son?

*****

Lei entered her parents' home early in the afternoon, this time accompanied by Yimin. She was glad she hadn't told her father about Yimin's erring ways. They had respected each other from the first time she had brought Yimin home. Her father admired the fact that Yimin had shared his sense of obligation to do well, explaining that his parents were supporting him financially and that one day he would return the favour. At that time he had still planned to go back to his father's village and apply for some government land to work with Dageng. He would use the technological skills he was learning at university to raise pigs scientifically, increasing their weight, life span and marketability. He planned to share all the knowledge he was learning at university with his father and brother.

Now, seated across from her father, Lei and Yimin presented a united front. Her mother fussed around pouring them small cups of green tea. Lei noticed how quiet her father was. She wanted to cry out, "Why didn't you help me?"

A shadow passed over the floor. They heard their dogs barking. They had tied them up in the back of the compound, knowing the dogs' hatred for Gang.

Gang approached the sliding door from the courtyard. She was alone, without her committee members.

Lei's mother didn't offer Gang any tea. She didn't invite her to sit down. Gang seated herself on a small stool near the doorway.

"First we talk," Gang said in a dictatorial voice. "We know you're pregnant, Lei. For a fee, I can arrange with someone to take you by boat to Bangkok where you will then go onto Australia on another ship. I can arrange for someone to meet you and get you both the right papers to stay and work there."

She paused and looked directly at Lei. "Your father and mother have agreed to pay half the fee and you and Yimin must pay one-quarter of it now and the last quarter will be collected from your wages in Australia. You can take Kai with you if Yimin's parents will let him go. I warn you though, it's a dangerous journey."

"Why are you doing this?" Lei interrupted. "Are you a snakehead?"

"That's none of your business."

Lei looked at Yimin with a question in her eyes. Was this a safe alternative? What about the plan they'd prepared with his Aunty? Could they truly survive in another country? They both had university degrees but would they be recognized in Australia? What about Yimin's English? Could he survive there? Would they be able to educate their children? How would she manage without the support of her mother and mother-in-law? And who would look after her parents later if they were gone?

She looked from her father to her mother. Her eyes met her mother's and she could tell by the strain on her face that she had spent many hours talking with her father to convince him that this way was the right decision. Lei and Yimin and their children would escape from the Communist party that dictated everything, even this intimate area of their married lives. The Party never questioned how the One Child Policy was being policed, and at what cost to the women of China.

But what would happen to her parents after they left the country? Would they be punished?

"Why would you do this? How can you protect Mama and Papa from being punished if we leave China?" she questioned.

"Leave that to my father. He has contacts in high places. He can protect them. We will give my father some of your money."

"How much will it cost?" Lei heard Yimin ask.

"It will be thirty-five thousand up front, thirty-five thousand after you reach Australia."

Yimin interrupted, "Is this RMB or Australian funds?"

"Australian funds."

Both Yimin and Lei mentally counted the meager savings they had managed to put aside to survive the future obligations that would dictate their lives in China. It was nowhere near the almost five hundred thousand RMB that Gang was asking for.

"There will be people in Sydney who will lend you money

when you arrive. You just have to find the two hundred and forty-five thousand RMB before you leave." Gang spoke as if they had already agreed. "Be at the wharf in Ningbo this Friday at six a.m. with one suitcase and the money. There will be room for the three of you. Bring some food."

As Gang turned and limped away, Lei wondered what had changed Gang's mind. What made her offer them this deal? Was it related to the secret her mother knew?

Lei and Yimin were left alone to decide their fate. Could they bring themselves to borrow such a huge sum of money? Or was it that Gang now knew that Lei's uncle had left her mother some foreign money in Australia when he died? Had her mother used this information to bargain with Gang?

Yimin and Lei told her parents how little money they had saved up. All their earnings were going to Yimin's family to pay back his university debt. They questioned Lei's mother about how they could get access to the money left to her by her brother in Australia. She had no answer for them, but assured her Gang had ways of tracking down people, especially if money was involved.

Lei tugged at Yimin's arm. "If we are really going to

go, I want to talk to Cezanne. She was married to an Australian."

Her father moved uncomfortably on his stool. It was obvious he wasn't convinced that leaving was a good idea. Lei's mother seemed more confident. She had a dream that Lei and Yimin and Kai could live in a free country. The final decision was to trust Gang, in the hope that the large sum of money she was asking for would deter her from betraying them.

Yimin decided to go to his parents to see if they might add more funds.

They would not be meeting together in this courtyard again. Lei looked one last time on the familiar scene, then shook her head as if to empty it of doubt.

Alone in her dormitory, Lei paced the floor. Could she give up her studies, leave China and take Kai away from his grandparents? How would Yimin survive in a foreign country without a better command of English?

Her thoughts were interrupted by her phone ringing.

"Yes, Yimin, I'm at my dormitory now and will see Cezanne tomorrow. Where are you? Have you seen your parents? We may have to insist they let us take Kai. Kiss him for me. And remember, no wine with your dad."

# CHAPTER 17

That evening, Yimin sat with his father in their outside courtyard.

"But Papa, I told you I'm not going to drink anymore, just some tea will do."

"Come on son, this is the sweet wine left over from Spring Festival. Your mother has heated it up."

"No Papa, I am determined not to drink anymore. I promised Lei."

"That's crazy son, why would you do that?"

"Because Papa, when I drink I can't remember what I do."

"But you're not going to have too much tonight."

Yimin's mother came into the room, carrying steaming hot dumplings on a platter.

"See," said his father. "Have some dumplings with the wine. They will digest together," he insisted.

Yimin took a freshly made dumpling but avoided the wine in front of him.

"If you're not drinking with your father, come in the kitchen and make dumplings with Kai and me," said his mother.

"Yes Papa, come," Kai called out.

Yimin entered the small kitchen. Kai was standing beside his grandmother, both hands and the front of his clothing dusted with flour. A bowl of freshly made dough rested on the counter. A wicker tray balanced between the counter and the stove. It was already laden with completed dumplings waiting to be steamed.

"Want some help, son?" Yimin gently edged Kai further around the short counter.

Kai's eyes lit up when he discovered his father would help. They each pinched a small portion of the dough from the bowl and rolled it between their hands until it was perfectly round and still shiny, not sticky. Kai got sidetracked and started to make a snake with his dough. Yimin placed his round ball on a plate and pinched another portion. His mother took the completed ball from the plate and threw it down on her small wooden board. Using a small rolling pin she flattened the dough, turning it lightly several times to make it perfectly round. She slid it to the side and took another ball to roll. Yimin picked up the thin circle of dough and held it flat in his left palm, while his right hand used chopsticks to lift a small portion of the fragrant pork filling from a glass bowl nearby. Flakes of Chinese cabbage and green onion dotted the mixture. Putting the lump in the middle of the circle of dough, he folded it in half with his chopsticks and proceeded to use his fingers to pinch the edges together in little pleats. He gently laid the completed dumpling on the woven bamboo tray with the other one hundred or so his mother had already made.

Kai concentrated on his wiggly snake.

"You know your father and I don't agree with you going to Australia. I have already told Dageng and Qing about Lei's baby. They want it. You must explain this to Lei. You must make her see that this is the best way."

They worked together in silence for the next half hour.

"Time to cook some more," his mother said, a strained smile on her face as Yimin stood back to let her use her chopsticks to pick up about twenty dumplings one by one and drop them into the large pot on her gas stove element. The hot steam drifted out the open window. The bubbling water returned to the boil, making the dumplings rise from the bottom of the pan and float around near the surface. When they were all floating his mother used her large strainer spoon to skim them off the surface and into a serving bowl.

"Here Kai, take these to your grandpa."

Yimin followed Kai into the other room, proud of the way his son concentrated on his task. Kai took his place at the table.

"Put them in the empty bowl Kai," his grandfather instructed.

"Pass me the dipping sauce. Son, why are you trusting Gang? It's unwise to play along with her. She is bound to trick you. Can't Lei stay here and go into hiding to have the baby?"

"I promised Lei I would do this, Papa. She won't agree to give the baby to Dageng and Qing. You said you have contacts in Australia that could help us when we get there. Tell me about them."

"Your great grandfather's brother went to Australia

when they needed miners there for the big Gold Rush. He kept the family name of Lee. It has been a long time since anyone has heard of him but we were told he became a wealthy man. If you could find his family I am sure they would help you. If you go, we will send a letter of introduction with you."

"But how could we find them in such a big country?" asked Yimin. "I do know that my boss at the factory says the owner of our factory now lives in Sydney and he has three children. I have never met him but I hear they call him an 'astronaut' because he can fly between Australia and China. The Chinese community in Australia helped him get the legal papers to stay in the country."

His father interrupted. "Can't you see this is a foolish scheme? Your degree was in agriculture and our plan was always for you to work together with Dageng and me on our land. You should all move back to the countryside like we planned."

"Father, we want to get away from China and start a new life."

Resignation in his voice, Yimin's father added, "If you do really go, you're not taking Kai. It's too dangerous. If it does work out, we will consider if you can take him later."

"You know they would never let us back if we leave."

"Well then, don't leave. Stick to your mother's plan and give the baby to Dageng."

His mother interrupted them, her strong gaze not faltering. "It is the best plan, Yimin."

They ate in silence. Even Kai seemed to know it was best to keep quiet.

They finished their meal and then drank a bowl of the warm dumpling soup. Kai wanted his father to sleep over but Yimin had to go back to the factory to work an evening shift.

Moonlight shone on his mother's greying hair as she said goodbye to him at the gate.

"Think about it Yimin. It's best if you convince Lei of her duty."

"I told you Mama, we are going to accept Gang's plan. Lei's family has some money in Australia and now you are saying we have a relative there. We will use everyone's savings to pay the first amount. Lei's parents will help. Why won't you help?"

"Because we will need our money to raise Kai." She paused and raised her voice without making eye contact.

"If you leave you will not be taking Kai."

"Yes, we will." He raised his voice over his mother's.

"We leave this Sunday morning and Lei and I will be here to get him after dark on Saturday. Make sure he is ready with a bag of warm clothes. Don't tell anyone."

Kai left his grandfather's side and ran to his father. He stood between his father and grandmother, pulling on his father's pant leg.

"Don't fight, Papa."

"We're not fighting, Kai. I'm just telling your grandmother what we are doing. Your mother and I will come and get you on Saturday night. Be ready."

# CHAPTER 18

Yimin and Lei sat on the bed in his dormitory. "Do you think we will be safe on the boat?" Lei asked.

"I can't say Lei, I don't like boats. I've only fished from the shore. This will be many weeks at sea."

"I'm afraid," Lei said, her body hunched as she sat cross legged in the middle of his bed.

"There is the other way, Lei. My mother says if you would go with Qing to her hometown in Hainan and keep in hiding, then when you had the baby, you could give it to Qing and no one would know it wasn't hers."

"Your mother planned this already?"

"Yes, and Dageng agreed."

There was silence for a moment.

"No, I told you I can't give it up. Your aunty said it is

a chance for us to allow our baby to live and that's exactly how I feel."

"Isn't that being selfish, Lei? We already have our son. Isn't he enough?"

Yimin wanted to go and look for a drink. Lei sensed his restlessness and left to get him a cola at the canteen downstairs. It gave her time to think about what he was saying. She felt betrayed. Why couldn't he let go of his mother's plan?

She stopped by the communal toilet to vomit. Morning sickness was beginning to be a regular thing.

"You promised," she said as she returned with the cola. In exasperation her voice was almost begging as she added, "I thought you understood how important this was to me, and to Kai, to all of us."

"I do, but I know my sister-in-law has been waiting a long time for a son."

"How do you know it will be a son? It might be a girl, but I don't care. I love it already." She glanced down at her belly, hidden under her baggy clothing. She felt stronger, standing up for this baby's life.

Yimin paced the room as if looking for a way to escape.

Finally he sat down beside Lei.

"If you are sure this is what you want, we will do it. But it will be dangerous for Kai. We must consider if we should leave him here until we are settled."

Lei went to speak and he cut her short. "Not now, we will decide tomorrow."

They lay in the bed, each alone with their own thoughts.

Lei realized it was the first time she had actually said no to Yimin. Well, she would also say no to Kai being left behind. If they were going to start a new life it would be all together, not apart.

Dreams of the future gave her respite at last.

A nightingale sang as they slept.

# CHAPTER 19

Cezanne sat with Lei in her room. "I can't understand why you are doing this, Lei. It's dangerous. You don't even know how to swim."

"I have to do this if I want to keep my baby." Lei sat down on the bed and rocked her body like a mother cradling her infant.

Cezanne moved closer and put her arms around Lei's shoulders. "She's a snakehead, Lei. Be careful. There are terrible stories of Asians who never reach their destination on these boats, some crash on reefs before they get there. If they do make it to Australia, they are arrested for illegal entry. They spend years in detention because of these snakeheads."

The enthusiasm that had shown on Lei's face drained

away. "Surely our case will be different because my mother says her family has some money in Australia. Once we get there, we can use that money to get established. Yimin has been talking to his boss and has found out that the owner of his factory now lives in Sydney. Maybe he can help us when we get there."

"That may be Lei, and I have heard of some refugees who have been given asylum because of the human rights issues around your One Child Policy. I still think it is too dangerous a trip for you, especially with Kai. The fee is exorbitant too. She is going to keep it all for herself. I can't believe your parents would help you with this scheme."

"They are only doing it because they know I want to keep the baby. My father is afraid of what might happen to us if we stay in China and try to keep it. Yimin and his mother want me to have the baby and then give it to his sister-in-law, but I can't bear to do that."

"Of course you can't. But maybe that is the only safe thing to do."

Lei stood up and started packing her suitcase.

"I have another idea." Cezanne said. "Go to the Australian Consulate and apply to study there. The papers will be processed quickly, I think, if you tell them about your family having some contacts there. Once you are there you can have the baby born there and then apply to be a refugee, eventually sponsoring Yimin and Kai to join you. I'll go with you to the office today. We can talk to Ian. He has contacts in Sydney."

Lei pondered this idea. It sounded safer but she'd have to go alone and would she even qualify before she began to show too much? Already she knew there was a slight swelling of her belly. Yimin had stroked her abdomen last night and told her of his commitment to never drink again. She wasn't quite sure about that but was relieved when he added that he also would never have sex again with another woman. That was more important to her.

"I better talk to Yimin about this plan," Lei said to Cezanne. "We have already made arrangements to meet Gang at the shipyard on Sunday. My family is trying to raise the first installment of the money now."

"Okay, do what you have to do, but let's go online and check out the Study in Australia application."

Lei booted up her laptop and went to the Australian foreign student's form. It seemed straightforward.

"Let's call and make an appointment to see the consulate tomorrow," Cezanne urged.

Dialing the number, Cezanne allowed Lei to brush her long blond hair. Lei never ceased to be fascinated by its translucent colour. The texture was such a contrast to her short black lengths that surrounded her face like a cap.

Her thoughts were interrupted as she heard Cezanne speak into the phone. "Yes, she would be a married student. It would just be to finish her last year of her master's degree. Oh, I see. Well, we will get back to you.

"Shit, Lei, they say if you are married you have to have a pregnancy test before they will consider your application."

"Back to plan A then," Lei said in almost a whisper. "I think I will just lie down for awhile. I'm feeling, what is it you and Ian say, 'on overload.' Is that right?"

"Yes, I can imagine you are. Just rest and try to forget about finding a solution right now. You are expecting, you know, and need special treatment." She started to massage Lei's feet as Lei settled herself on the bed.

"I can't wait to be an Aunty again!"

# CHAPTER 20

"You can't take him," his mother said as Yimin attempted to bundle Kai up in a quilt. Lei stuffed his few clothes into a rucksack.

Yimin managed to get Kai settled on his hip with the quilt wrapped around him. It was still dark.

"Talk to Aunty Mei, Mama, she knows why we are doing this."

"No. You must leave him here. You can send for him." Yimin's mother pulled at the quilt trying to make him give up Kai.

"We can't leave without him," Lei said as Yimin transferred Kai to her arms. Kai's chubby little hands went around her neck as she held him close. She was talking more to herself than to her mother-in-law.

Suddenly Yimin's mother grabbed Kai from Lei and ran to her husband's cart that was waiting outside the lean-to door.

Yimin held Lei back. She wrestled frantically with him, as she saw his mother climb inside the cart with Kai. Yimin's father pedaled away, as Kai cried out for Yimin and Lei, but the cart was soon lost to sight in the street full of early morning commuters.

Lei sobbed and pounded Yimin's chest as he held her in his arms. His voice was breaking with pain as he tried to reason with her. "Lei, We can't put Kai in danger. We must leave him. Forgive me, please forgive me. I love you both."

"I can't go without Kai."

"We must. This is the only way."

"But Gang said to bring him. Others have done it before us. Remember she said we will be met by some people when we transfer to a smaller boat to land on the shore of Australia. They will help us get papers to stay in Sydney." Lei was trying to convince herself. She knew Yimin was right. It was too dangerous a trip for Kai.

"Remember, she said we will have to work for some foreigners she knows. When we pay the last fee we can go on our own. We can even send for our parents when they are old."

Yimin was thinking about these promises, and then he reminded her of Gang's last words: "Tell no one of this plan, except your family, or I will take you to the hospital for an abortion, this time with the police."

"There was so much hatred in her eyes. No wonder she walks like a vulture. She is one," he said.

Lei's mind raced with thoughts; What had caused this hatred and greed? Was ripping babies out of women's wombs a way to show her loyalty to the Party rules or was it a way to collect all their money? What about Gang's own child who her parents wouldn't accept? Did she know that its harelip could be fixed? Lei's mother had told her the child would soon be sold to a couple in Germany.

A light went on in her mind. Did Gang know about this and want her back? Had her mother traded information for help?

# CHAPTER 21

The next day, Cezanne was up early. She showered and ate a banana with her morning tea. She was worried about Lei's final decision to go to Australia. Was it a set up? Could it possibly be that Gang would be true to her word and get them safely to Australia? What then? The only sure thing seemed to be that Gang would get her money up front.

Cezanne entered the Qigong class a bit late. The students were already on their first routine. It was 6:00 a.m. Sunday morning.

Ian winked at Cezanne. His body and head remained fluid as he moved almost hypnotically from one pose to another. Ian had told Cezanne that this was why he had come to China. He wanted to become a Qigong Master.

"What do you really do?" she had asked him one night after their date was interrupted by many cell calls which he took in private or seemed to respond to in riddles.

"I work at the restaurant and study Qigong," he said. "You know that."

"Well, why so many calls? Do you really have that many friends I don't know?"

"You're very inquisitive and cute," he had said, not answering her question. She noticed that the calls diminished on their subsequent dates.

Cezanne was anxious to share Lei's decision with Ian, even though Lei had asked her to tell no one. She wanted to ask him about his contacts in Sydney. She was sure they would help Lei and Yimin.

After class they went across the street and sat outdoors at a small table with a hotpot steaming in the middle. They slowly chose mushrooms, bok choy and thinly sliced sweet potatoes from the raw vegetable cart that was beside their table. Some of the live baby shrimp escaped their basket and started crawling on the table as Ian used his chopsticks to pick up two or three of them and drop them back into the steaming water.

"Lei and Yimin are going to leave today," she said as

he ate a prawn.

"Where to?" he asked in surprise.

"Sydney, Australia. By ship. It's all set up by this horrid official who's been trying to get Lei to have an abortion."

"What ship are they going on and what's it costing them?" Ian asked abruptly.

"I don't know exactly. It seems they pay some now and some when they get to Australia and they can work the rest off while they are there."

"That's bullshit! What ship did they say they are sailing on?"

"I think it's one of the ones at the pier now because they have to board this morning at 8:00 a.m. I think it leaves at 10 a.m. Lei says it goes to Bangkok first and then they change to another boat for the long route to Australia."

"They mustn't go, Cezanne. To be granted asylum in Australia, they will have to go into detention first before their case will even be considered." He took a breath. "I think I know the boat you mean. It's going north, not south. It's a rip-off. They'll never see their money again and maybe lose their lives. Have they given their money yet or the name of the Australian contact?"

"No, I think they do that when they get to the ship. They didn't want me to go and say good-bye because it is all underground."

"I've got to stop them. This plan is suicide. I know a way to the dock that should get me there in time."

Ian got up from the table and started to leave. "You wait at the dormitory and I'll call you when I get them off the ship if they have already boarded."

"No, wait for me. I'm coming too, I'm afraid of what that Gang woman will do to Lei if they back out now. I'm afraid she will make her have an abortion."

## CHAPTER 22

Cezanne followed Ian down a crowded alleyway, passing vendors and avoiding garbage. He stopped at what looked like a manhole and removed the heavy iron covering.

Before he headed down, he asked her, "Are you sure you want to come? This could be nasty."

"Yes, let's hurry."

To her surprise there were iron stairs leading directly down to a dirt floor below. She followed close behind him, her eyes adjusting to the dark. He produced a small flashlight and led the way, through many interconnecting cell-like rooms, stocked with boxes and containers. Was this part of the wharf materials or was it part of the underground city she had read about years ago? The underground roads were built in the years from 1969 to

1979 in the major Chinese cities after China and Russia were no longer allies. She had read that in Beijing one such underground city could hold up to eight or nine million people in the event of a nuclear attack.

"Wait," she called to Ian as he raced ahead. A monstrous rat scurried across her path and she screamed. He glanced back but kept going.

"Catch up," he called . "We must stop them!"

Finally the darkness ahead lessened. Light streamed through a huge grated gate onto the pier at Ningbo's large vessel wharf. Cezanne took in the busy scene as she pushed herself to keep pace with Ian. Small punts were rafted alongside each other at the wharves. Families hung their laundry out on poles from the decks. Birds squawked and swooped down as fish were being gutted.

Cezanne wondered how they would know which ship was the right one? Ian kept going, past big container ships, past a cruise ship.

"There it is," he shouted, pointing to a rusty vessel on the next wharf. The crew was loading barrels of something onto its deck and Cezanne could see Yimin and Lei with their suitcases just going on board. Gang was nowhere to be seen.

"Get off," Ian yelled.

Yimin and Lei turned at the sound of Ian's familiar voice. His Mandarin was not the best but he must have said what he wanted to say as not only Yimin and Lei stopped but also the workers.

Ian leaped up the gangplank and called to Yimin and Lei to follow him off the boat. They were confused and didn't know what to do. When they saw Cezanne on the wharf, motioning them to come, they followed him.

As soon as they were on the wharf, Ian demanded, "Where's the money?"

"We've given it to Gang about a half hour ago. She's gone now," replied Yimin.

"Yes, and so is your money. This boat is not going anywhere near where she says it is. You will be let out in Thailand and left on your own to survive. You'll probably end up in a Bangkok jail. You must believe me, I know what I'm talking about."

"How do you know?" Yimin asked.

"Trust me, Yimin," Ian's low, urgent voice included the three of them.

"For your own safety, I didn't want to tell you that I work for an American company which susses out pirates at sea. The multinational companies can't afford the high insurance needed to sail in international waters, so they hire people from companies like mine who have ships patrolling the sea using very sophisticated technology. They're on the lookout for dangerous vessels."

"So, that's what all those mysterious phone calls were about?" Cezanne interjected.

Lei and Yimin followed Ian's words with growing comprehension and relief at their narrow escape.

"This vessel has been known to approach smaller vessels at sea and put their crews afloat while they take all their cargo. The Chinese government knows about this but turns a blind eye. They make like they will prosecute the culprits but they never do." He added, "It's a corrupt group of people we are dealing with."

"But what about our money?" Yimin asked.

Lei and Cezanne embraced each other against the chill of the morning air. Cezanne wrapped her coat protectively around both of them. Ian's attention shifted to Yimin.

"We will have to go and confront Gang."

Ian was thinking out loud. "If she sees that I am onto her, she may give it back. Otherwise I think you should leave and head to the countryside until the baby is born, then Cezanne and I will do everything we can to sponsor you out of the country. This is no way to live."

They headed back through the crowds that had gathered around them. Ian took time to do his best to tell the others on the boat to get off.

"It's not going where they promised you," he said in perfect Mandarin.

Disillusioned eyes looked pleadingly up at him, as if they expected him to decide their next step.

"Get off," he said. "Go to whoever took your money and try to get it back. I can't help you. Leave now before the officials discover your plans."

*****

Back at the dormitory, Lei and Yimin sat in silence. Finally, Yimin got up and warmed some noodles on the little one burner coal stove. "Have some noodles." He said when they were warm.

"No, they'll just make me vomit."

"Are you still having morning sickness?" Yimin asked, the tenderness in his voice, evident.

Ignoring his question, Lei asked, "What do you think we should do?"

"I hope we can get all the money back. Mama and

Papa were right, we should never have trusted Gang. I wonder why your mother did?"

"Mama knows something about Gang's past. Gang better watch out. When my Mama gets mad she really gets mad."

Yimin ignored her comment and reminded her of their need to meet Ian and Cezanne in front of the Neighbourhood Committee office as soon as possible.

"Maybe your Mama should come with us, and then I think we should go and see if Kai is okay. You rest first while I eat."

As Yimin ate, Lei tried to sleep but questions still mushroomed in her head. Why was all this happening? Why couldn't she find a way to keep this baby herself? Why must she always follow other peoples' plans?

Tossing and turning, she fell into a fretful sleep. She awoke to her own voice shouting, "Give him back." Her inner thighs burned where the baby had emerged from her womb and rested for only a second before Qing grabbed it and pressed it to her own chest.

Yimin was beside her instantly. "I'm here," he said. "I told you I won't let them take the baby from you."

Lei sobbed in his arms. Why did she feel so alone?

# CHAPTER 23

They met as agreed in the little noodle restaurant across the street from the Neighbourhood Committee office. As always the blond foreigners attracted attention. When Ian left the group, the customers stopped eating, their eyes widening with surprise as he crossed over to the Neighbourhood Committee office. Cezanne kept her hand in Lei's even as the pressure of Lei's grip became painful.

"I want to see Gang," Ian called out to the clerk who was loitering in the doorway, smoking a cigarette.

"She's left. Taken some girl to the clinic. She won't be back today."

"Oh yes she will!" Cezanne heard Ian shout in Mandarin. "And if I have my way she'll be behind bars before nightfall. This is inhumane and corrupt. How can she serve two masters, the government and herself? Her superiors won't be pleased to hear she is collecting double money, not only the fines but also payoff money for her phony trips to Australia."

This was quite a long speech in Mandarin for Ian and at the mention of Australia, two men in police uniforms appeared. Ian opened his jacket lapel and showed them some kind of official badge which served to impress them.

Suddenly, Cezanne glimpsed Gang disappearing up the street behind the office. "There she is!" Cezanne shouted from the door of the restaurant.

Ian quickly led the chase, with the two police officers close on his heels. Gang's shuffling was no match for their long, strong strides.

Ian grabbed Gang's wrists and pulled them behind her back. Handcuffs appeared from inside his jacket and he clicked them onto her wrists.

Gang yelled abuse. Passersby stopped to watch and listen as Ian pulled her away. He flagged a taxi. The driver looked doubtingly at Ian's captive.

One of the policemen tried to stop him, "You can't

take her away."

"Just try to stop me," said Ian. "To the City Wharf Guards Office!" he shouted to the driver, maintaining his hold as he forced Gang into the backseat.

Ian frowned, but said nothing when he saw Cezanne get into the front seat with the driver.

Fending off Gang's blows, Ian rolled down the window, "Meet back at the courtyard of your dorm, Yimin. We'll be there as soon as I finish with this."

## CHAPTER 24

"You must make a statement, Lei," Cezanne was saying. "This woman is evil and we must stop her from doing more terrible things to other women."

Lei knew Cezanne was right but she also knew that her family and Yimin's would suffer if she exposed Gang. And Kai, would he be safe?

Ian sat beside her as if to reassure her he would be there for her. She wanted to cooperate. Yimin moved closer too.

Lei felt her breath become rhythmic. She found herself thinking objectively. How to avoid incriminating herself and involving her whole family?

It was Ian who thought of a way around it. "Deny being pregnant. Just say that Gang was hounding you to go to the abortion clinic without any proof. Tell them that you and Yimin just wanted to leave the country for a better life." Lei sat at the picnic table screened by the other three. While they discussed the situation she wrote with concentration. In a few minutes she folded the completed letter and gave it to Ian.

"Wait, Lei," her mother said as she appeared at the gateway to the courtyard. She was followed by her father.

Her mother lowered her voice and whispered in Lei's ear, "You and Yimin go back. Leave this to your father and me. We came to warn you that Gang's committee is looking for you to insist you have a pregnancy test immediately. Gang wants to have proof that you were leaving because of the pregnancy. The officials will overlook the money issue but they will enforce your obedience to the state's law. There are more people involved in this than Gang. They are sure to release her."

"But what about your money?"

"Forget about it now, and get to safety. Take Kai with you, he may be in danger too. Leave now and your father and I will deliver your statement."

"Come Lei, do as your mother says," Yimin pulled at her sleeve as he headed in the direction of Ian and

Cezanne who had started to leave.

"I'll stay with you," said Cezanne, leaving Ian and turning back to Lei. "I can help you pack."

"No need to pack," urged Yimin. "We can take exactly what we have now. We have to go to Kai."

Lei's face suddenly contorted and her knees buckled.

"Lei," Yimin cried springing to her side and lifting her limp body. "Lei," he repeated in a whisper, cradling her to his chest. Lei felt her strength returning as she heard the love in his voice.

Her mother wiped her forehead with a handkerchief. "Take her away now. This has been too much for her."

Yimin had to push his way through the crowd that had gathered. Cezanne flagged down a cab for them, her eyes showed the compassion that was too deep to voice. Yimin gently lay his wife on the back seat. Ian put their suitcase in the trunk and told the driver to take them to the bus station.

"You stay with me, Cezanne, they are better off on their own. Get another taxi, we are going with Lei's parents to the Harbour Guard House." Grimly, he added, "I hope they are still holding Gang."

Arriving several minutes later he demanded, "Where

is she?" The Guard House was empty except for a small group guards playing mahjong. The click of their tiles smacking the tabletop was the only sound.

"I left that woman with you. Where is she?" Ian opened his wallet to show the company ID card which he'd used earlier.

"She left soon after you did," one guard replied, continuing to concentrate on his game. "Think she went home."

"But I told you to lock her up till I came back."

"Did you?" the other guard stood, taller and stockier than Ian. "I don't recall you saying that. Best get out of here before we hold you for trespassing on government property."

Ian could see he wasn't going to get anywhere. "You two leave now," he uttered in a low voice to Lei's mother and father. "It's probably best if you stay out of this as much as possible. Not sure how we're going to get your money back. Guess that is the least of our worries right now."

"You're right, Ian. Let's go, Siewling," Lei's father guided his wife to the doorway. Once outside the building he added, "Best we don't say anything about all this. Let Lei and Yimin get away first." It was as if her father's worst nightmare was happening to his daughter.

# CHAPTER 25

Lei's mother and father saw smoke rising above their gate as they approached their compound. People were crowded around the entrance.

"Aie! What has happened?"

The iron gate swung open, a hacksaw had been used to cut through the lock.

"Help me get some water," Lei's father yelled.

Neighbours were already arriving with buckets and rolling barrels of water through the gate. The concrete building was safe, but Lei's mother could see that all their possessions had been thrown into the yard and set on fire. Her husband's bicycle and all his medical supplies were piled with everything moveable from the house and little shed.

"Who did this?" Lei's father asked uselessly when the fire had died down.

"Your son-in-law's work unit were here looking for you this morning. They said your daughter is pregnant again without permission and planning to have the baby. Is that right?" one bystander asked accusingly.

Before they had a chance to answer, a nurse from her father's hospital said, "We tried to stop them, but they wouldn't stop. They said your daughter must have an abortion or pay the fine."

"Who says she's pregnant?" Lei's mother demanded. "She's never even had a test."

"Well, make her get one. She's made Yimin's work team lose their monthly wages and bonuses."

An elderly neighbour put her arm around Lei's mother. "Come away, Siewling. Rest at our home. I don't think they will come back."

"But what about Yimin and Lei? Will they be safe?" Lei's mother asked in a whisper.

The neighbor spoke up. "I'm afraid for them. Gang came after the work crew. She swore she would find Lei and make her pay the fine or go to the clinic. She said she had some other unfinished business with you and Lei. Do you know what she meant?"

The crowd in the yard squeezed closer to hear Lei's mother's reply. She ignored the question and said, "How can we pay the fine? Gang already has all our money."

"Shush," said her husband. "That was supposed to be done in secret. Don't tell everyone." His hand on her shoulder guided her as they followed the old woman through the meddlesome crowd.

## CHAPTER 26

On the bus, Lei found herself breaking out in perspiration as the reality of her situation loomed in front of her. A voice inside her spoke clearly, "The only way now to save this baby is to promise it to Qing and Dageng."

Tears mingled with the dust on her cheeks.

Oh little one, can you forgive me? It's the only way I can save you. They will find a safe place for us to hide. Her people are Miao people and the officials don't monitor them. As hard as it will be for me to do this, it is the only safe way to keep you. I will make Qing and Dageng promise me they will tell you the truth when you are older. You will know one day that I am your mother.

She continued to cry silently when she realized the

decision she was being forced to make.

"Relax," Yimin said as he tightened his arm around her shoulders. "Have you decided?" he asked gently.

"Yes," she choked out. "The only way is to give it to Qing and Dageng. But they must agree to let us tell the child when it is older. It must know that I am its real mother and that we only did this because there was no other way,"

There was a sadness between them that no words could temper.

Finally, Yimin asked, "Will the school let you keep your job if you leave university now, Lei? I know my boss will sack me if I leave."

Silence again.

Lei prepared herself for what she knew he was going to say. She impulsively pushed the collar of her coat up over her ears in an attempt to prevent hearing his voice.

"Could you go alone with Qing?" he moved closer as he spoke.

"Kai and I could stay here with my parents and Dageng. We could tell anyone who asked that you had to go with Qing to her home village in Hainan, to be with her while she birthed her child. I could keep my job and you could have yours back when you returned."

Lei slouched forward, resting her forehead on the seat in front. Could she go through with this plan? Did she have the strength to go against the government and deceive everyone? She recalled the story of her ancestor cutting his queue and felt a surge of determination, answering her own question.

"Yes, I will do it," she said softly, so no one on the bus could hear her. "If this is what I must do to let you live, then I will."

Gone was the indecision. Suddenly it was black and white. Life and death. If this was the only way she could keep her baby, then so be it. The baby must live. Her thoughts produced an idiom her foreign friends were teaching her, "It is what it is." It seemed to fit her situation and choices. When she descended from the bus her decision was firm.

Once off the bus and walking towards the house, Lei called out, "Kai! Kai!"

Entering the compound, she saw him playing with Qing by the water pump. Their cheeks were flushed with chilblains. Qing's hands were red and swollen as they washed the bok choy in the freezing well water.

"Oh Kai, come here quickly," Lei said as she ran up and snatched him away from his play. "We must never leave you again." She embraced him like a lion rescuing its cub from danger. She wanted to hold him and protect him forever.

"Calm down, Lei." Yimin said. "He's been safe here with Qing." He took her hand and motioned to her to leave Kai with Qing. "Come, we must tell my mother of our decision."

"First I must speak to Qing."

Walking over to the water pump where Qing was still washing vegetables, Lei knelt down close to her.

"Do you and Dageng really want this baby? Will you go away with me and make everyone think it is yours?"

"Yes, of course. Will you give it to us?"

"Only if you agree to tell it when it's older, that I am really its mother."

"Do you think that is wise?"

"It can be done in secret. No one needs to know except the child and us."

"I will talk to Dageng and see if he will agree. It's really my mother-in-law's idea, not ours. But Lei, if you do this, I promise I will love it as if it were my own."

"I don't want you to love it more than I do, that's what I am afraid of." Lei spoke with earnest.

Yimin broke in, "Let's not wait any longer, Lei. Let's find my mother and tell her your decision. You both must get ready to leave."

"Yes." Qing agreed, "We should go as soon as possible. If you are not here they will have no evidence of your pregnancy."

Lei spoke up, "First I want you to find Dageng and get him to agree to my request. I won't do it unless you both promise to tell the child the truth one day."

*****

Qing found Dageng in the field with his father. Dageng walked behind the water buffalo, the blade of the ground hoe turning the soil. She motioned to him to stop. They moved to the raised path of the earth trench between the rows. While he was eating the lunch Qing had prepared for him, Qing told him of Lei's request.

"Will you agree?" she asked him.

"You know I don't like my mother's idea. I think we should wait another year. It's your duty to birth my son."

"But Dageng, this will help Yimin and Lei too, otherwise Gang will take the baby from her. I will still have another baby one day. Remember the law doesn't apply to me."

"I know, that's why I thought we would have four children by now. What is wrong with you?" His voice resounded accusingly.

"If I knew, then I would fix it, but I don't. Maybe we have displeased the gods. I burn incense to Guan Yin every chance I get. What do you do? Nothing except threaten me with divorce. Is that what your mother tells you to do?"

"How do you know that?"

"Your neighbour told me your mother told her," she said defiantly. "Divorce me if you must, but here is an easier solution. Take Yimin's child and we can make it our own."

"How will it be our own if she wants to tell it the truth?"

"Why can't we just agree, and then maybe we won't have to tell it. Who knows what the future holds?"

"I'll agree. But tell them I only want it if it's a boy. We know you can make a girl. If this is another girl, they can find a way to keep it themselves or give it to an orphanage."

"Dageng, girl or not, we don't want to give it to an

orphanage. That is no life, only a life of crime or prostitution comes from that when they grow up."

"Enough," said Dageng. "Go and get yourself ready. But be careful, only associate with your own people in Hainan. Don't let any spies see that it is Lei who is pregnant and not you."

# CHAPTER 27

"You'll be a good boy won't you Kai?"

"Papa will stay with me, right Mama?"

"Yes, Kai, and when Aunty Qing and I come back, we will bring a new baby brother or sister for you. Maybe you can pick a name."

"Will Grandma and Grandpa go with you?"

"No, they will stay and look after you. But I promise you, Kai, when we come back, your Papa and I are going to look after you always. We will all live together, I promise you."

Lei had done a lot of thinking since their narrow escape from the ship. She was determined to do everything in her power to keep Yimin and Kai as close as possible. She already had plans to study her university courses on-line while she waited in Hainan to birth the baby. She was beginning to think of talking Yimin into returning to the land and working with his family after the baby was born. It would mean they could all be together.

She fretted about how to retrieve the money her parents had lost. She had no answer and knew that Yimin and Ian would be pursuing this goal while she was away. Was it possible or was it too dangerous? She remembered the look on her father's face as he took her mother away from the confrontation with the men at the Neighbourhood Committee office.

Lei was sorry that her parents had become involved. She was determined not to implicate them any further. It was best not to return to their house. Her story of going with Qing to birth her baby in Hainan was more plausible. But she regretted she would not be able to see her mother one more time before leaving on this journey.

"Sleep with Grandma now, Kai. Your father and I must leave very early. Aunty Qing will come with us. Remember, she will bring home a new baby for you to play with."

"Don't go, Mama, I want to play with you and Papa."

"We will play soon, when I come back. Sleep now,

son."

When the house was quiet, Lei and Yimin asked Qing what Dageng's decision had been.

"He agrees, but he only wants it if it's a boy." Qing said almost apologetically.

"My brother said that, after all these years of waiting for a child?"

"Yes, but he did agree to let us tell the child the truth when he is older. You still think that is wise, Lei?"

"Yes, I thought you agreed."

Yimin's cell rang and he glanced at the caller ID before answering it. He slipped it back into his pocket.

"Who was that?"

"Someone from work, but I don't want them to know where we are."

"Are you sure?"

"What do you mean?" They moved to the kitchen where Qing couldn't hear them.

"Have you told that girl you won't see her again? What if she chases you while I am gone?"

"She won't. I've told her I was drunk and it didn't mean anything. Anyway I have a sponsor now. Remember Wang, my neighbour in the dormitory? He's also an AA member and we are going to as many meetings as we can fit in. There is one tonight in Cixi. If I get back in time we will go. If not, someone will call me to help me stay sober and away from girls like her."

"What about the nights you have to go drinking with the mother-in-laws? I am sure that girl won't give you up."

"I'll be drinking cola. I will be thinking clearly and avoid her. Trust me Lei."

Lei headed upstairs. She wanted to be alone for a few minutes.

Could she really trust Yimin? She was going to be so far away. What could she do if he started drinking again? Thoughts of the vulnerability of her situation flashed through her mind.

"Stop it!" she heard herself say. "Trust and pray." Wasn't that what her mother had said to her before they went to the boat? Trust and pray, God will be with you.

Ian had saved them from Gang's corrupt plot, so maybe her mother's god could protect them in Hainan.

Never mind, she continued, talking to herself, if he can't stay sober, I now have a plan. At least if it's a boy. If it turns out to be a girl I will need someone's help.

Her hand rested protectively on the slight swelling of her belly. She heard the cooing of her father-in-law's budgies as they settled down after he put their night cover over them.

You are safe inside me little one. Rest and grow strong.

# CHAPTER 28

Yimin and Lei rose before dawn the next morning. In spite of the early hour, the mist seemed to have its own light. Raindrops glistened on the drooping leaves of the willow trees outside the window.

They folded the quilts and stacked them against the wall on the bed. A lingering scent of their recent lovemaking filled the room.

"Hurry, Lei," they heard Qing's voice as she passed their bedroom on her way down the narrow stairs to the small kitchen below.

"Eat some congee," her mother-in-law said. "It's there in the bowl on the table. I'm making you some noodles to take with you on the train. Dageng has left already. He has to set the rice seedlings early today without the neighbors' help. They will miss your help," she said accusingly to Qing. "I wanted to tell them about your 'pregnancy' but Dageng says to wait. Why is this?"

"He only wants the baby if it's a boy," Qing said, more to the wall than to her mother-in-law. "He said to keep it a secret until we know the sex."

"Secret! Why should we keep it a secret, Qing? At his age, a baby is a baby. What do we care if it's a girl? I've heard that in Shanghai they are paying a bonus to couples who keep their girl babies. How else will all the young men find wives?"

"You're right, Mama, please talk to him."

"I will and I will have his father talk to him too. I am sure he will remind him of Confucius's ancient teaching about buying a child if no child is forthcoming."

"Are you ready, Qing?" Lei's voice broke into their conversation. "Yimin will take us to the train stop before daylight. I'm dreading the trip. Eighty-five hours to Zhanjiang, and then the ferry to Haikou. I'm tired already."

"Have you told your family we are coming?"

"No. Dageng thinks they may not like two of us coming. We will explain everything to them when we get there."

"Eat your congee, Lei," her mother-in-law repeated. "Remember you are eating for two now."

Lei bent and filled her bowl with the steaming watery rice from the pot atop the coal burner stove on the earthen floor. She sat on a small stool beside Qing. They ate in silence.

Using her chopsticks in her right hand, her free hand dropped to her belly. We are going to save you little one, she mused to herself as she straightened her back and pulled her womb into the protective hollow of her hips.

She finished her breakfast and slipped back up the stairs to her mother-in-law's room where Kai slept soundly in the warmth of their quilt. It would be several hours before Kai awoke and realized that Yimin and she were gone. Leaning over to kiss his flushed cheek, Lei wondered how she could be apart from him for so long. Would he forget her? Would he think she didn't love him anymore? Would Qing claim this child too?

She tucked the quilt tightly around him, turning the end under his feet. "Little one, I am doing this not just for me, but for you too. One day you will thank me for saving your little brother or sister." She stroked his small hand and felt his fingers encircle hers. She lingered with her kiss on his warm cheek.

Returning to the kitchen, Lei joined Yimin and witnessed him saying a formal good-bye to his mother. "We appreciate your help, Mama," she heard him say. The fear Lei had felt in her heart subsided when she heard her mother-in-law say tenderly to her son that Kai would be safe with them and they would be anxiously waiting for the arrival of the new little one.

Why couldn't she say that to me? Lei lamented. She brushed her negative thought aside. Be happy she said it to her son, she told herself.

*****

The wind whipped Lei's face as she straddled the scooter behind Yimin. The damp mist chilled her in spite of the heat from Yimin's body. Dageng had returned from the fields to get Qing.

Qing sat in the wagon attached to the bicycle that Dageng rode down the village path behind Yimin and Lei. Neither brother had communicated or looked at each other as they loaded the women up with vegetables and fruits rather than the costly gifts usually expected from visiting relatives. There had been no time or money for buying such things.

The train pulled into the station and the women climbed aboard. Yimin waved and Dageng watched silently as the train moved into the distance.

Yimin lifted his scooter onto Dageng's wagon. His shoulders fell as his brother peddled away without a word. Yimin turned and walked alone toward the bus station.

Work in the city awaited him.

# CHAPTER 29

Qing worked her way down the crowded aisle of the train. Lei followed. Their ticket, bought at the last minute, was a "standing only" ticket. But where to stand? There was nowhere.

Damp newspapers were scattered under the feet of those that were sitting. They smelled of the strong urine of the babies and toddlers who had peed on them during the night.

Qing spotted a man who stood to go somewhere. She lunged to grab his seat, squeezing her parcel on the bench beside her. Realizing what she had done, she removed the parcel to her lap and let the tired Lei sit down.

Hours later Lei wondered, Will I even survive this journey? She felt overwhelmed once again. The optimism she had felt was gone. She worried about being found on the train without a permit to move to another locality. Yimin had counseled her to say there wasn't anyone at the Police Station when she went to get the permission stamp. Tell them you both have to go to attend a funeral of one of Qing's relatives and as Qing is pregnant, she needs you. They will believe you because Qing is Miao and can return anytime to her home state, he had said.

"It will be alright. Relax and enjoy the scenery." Qing's voice broke into her thoughts.

Huge tracts of land stretched out from either side of the train. As the mist lifted, Lei could make out workers bending over in the fields. Sacks of rice seedlings hung from their shoulders. Deft hands placed the sprouted plants deep into muddy soil on the flooded land. A rhythmical sequence of bending and planting played out as labourers worked in unison. Their pointed straw hats covered their heads and shaded their shoulders. There was an aura of anonymity about them. Rice planting was foreign to Lei who had come from the north of China where wheat and soya beans were the staple crops.

The rattling of the train wheels soon lulled Lei to sleep. The anxiety of the past days drifted into oblivion. She rested her head on Qing's shoulder.

"Where's your moving permit?" an official demanded in the realm of her dream.

"I don't have one. I'm pregnant." Lei gasped as she woke up to her own voice.

"Shush," Qing said. "Do you want us to get detained?" People sitting near them leaned forward and waited for Lei to say more.

"It's okay," said Qing to the gawkers, "she's a bit delirious with the flu. She should have a face mask on." Qing opened her purse and produced a clean face mask which she pushed onto Lei's face.

"Wear this," she said with authority. "It will protect our fellow passengers." Satisfied, the onlookers adjusted themselves as far away from them as possible. They returned to their gossip and settled into their cramped quarters.

# CHAPTER 30

Rice paddies changed to concrete communities, devoid of planting fields. They merged one after another as the train rattled on. "Last stop," the conductor announced as they neared Zhanjiang, the seaport where they would catch the eight hour ferry ride to the city of Haikou on the north end of the island of Hainan.

"If you have a ticket for the ferry, present it to the bus driver in the station and he will deliver you to the ferry." A smile lit up the conductor's face as he recognized Qing.

"Are you coming home to stay?" he asked.

"No, to birth my baby," she said before she remembered that Dageng told her to keep their reason a secret.

"We're going to her auntie's funeral," Lei added, hoping he might have missed what Qing said.

"Blessings to the new baby," he responded as he walked away from them, continuing to announce his information.

"Who was that?" Lei asked.

"He is one of my uncles. His wife is a midwife. He will be sure to tell her what I said. Maybe they will help us. They live very close to my parents."

Qing stepped off the train and called back to Lei, "Hurry. We have to catch that ferry. It will be crowded."

Qing walked ahead of Lei, her path like a strand of weaving material making its way in and out of the congested people.

Lei stumbled over someone's foot and regained her balance just in time. "Wait, Qing, I can't keep up. Remember, I have never been here before and I'm tired. If I get lost I won't know where to go."

The diversity of the people ignited a new fear in Lei. Clusters of minority groups gathered together waiting for the ferry. The bright red and blue batik and tie-dyed clothing of the Li and Miao minority peoples was a contrast to the dull colours of the Han Chinese clothing.

She saw for the first time how intricate the minorities group silver jewelry was. She spotted a few people from Cambodia and Vietnam, their legs covered by their colourful wraparound pants known as sampots. Many women had white scarves, identifying themselves as belonging to the Hui minority group of Muslims in China. Qing had told her there were Muslim people in Hainan but she had never met one before. What did they think of China's One Child Policy? Would they report her if they found out she was the one pregnant and not Qing? She wondered who was to be feared?

"I told you there is nothing to worry about Lei." Qing said later, when they were settled on mats on the deck of the ferry.

"These Muslims just want to be free to practice their own faith. They do not want to talk to authorities. Many of them are here illegally. They just want to be left alone. Like us."

"Why do they wear the scarf then if they don't want to be noticed?"

"They believe they must hide their hair so as not to tempt men who are not their husbands."

I wish that woman Yimin slept with would wear

one, thought Lei. She should cover up her enticing hair. Lei didn't voice her thought. This was something she could never share with Qing.

"Come on now, sleep. We will arrive in Haiku early in the morning. My brother will meet us." Qing spread her thin quilt on the deck. They huddled close to each other for warmth.

*****

Dockyard noise woke Lei. The ship was already tied up at the wharf and cranes were lifting containers from its hold. Workers were calling out. Bananas had burst from one crate as it was clumsily transported over the water to a waiting truck on the wharf. Small boats swarmed to pick up the floating bananas.

"Qing." A masculine voice called out. "Over here."

"Brother, thank you for coming. We were going to take the bus."

"No need," he said as he took their bundles away from them and motioned for them to follow him.

"This is my sister-in-law, Lei. She will stay with us awhile." Lei sensed he knew she was not Miao.

"Why?" Bo asked. "Why have you brought her?"

"Our mother will tell you soon enough. Be happy to

see us."

"Yes, Sister, I am. Let's go. Our mother is waiting for you."

His truck-like vehicle, supported by one wheel in the front and two at the back, barely had room for all three of them to sit across the open-air bench seat. The carriage behind the seat was overloaded with freshly cut pig's ears.

Noticing Lei looking at the pork pieces, Bo explained "They are for the market in Sanya. We must hurry before the noon sun spoils them. I will take you to our compound first; it is just before Sanya at the south end of the island. It will be about a three hour drive."

Traffic in Haiku was like traffic in Cixi. They were both harbor cities. Their residents were familiar with tourist drivers, many of them bringing their cars to Hainan via the ferry. Bo wove deftly in and out of the traffic.

"There are three highways to Sanya," Qing's brother said. "We'll take the scenic one since your sister-in-law hasn't been here before. The road goes through the mountains and we will end up in our village near the Five Fingers Mountain." His friendliness eased Lie's anxiety. He was dressed in the typical Miao male clothing of dark cotton pants and a short black jacket. He smiled often, showing his row of blunt red stained teeth. Lei noticed him chewing on something and spitting successively out the truck window.

"Is your brother chewing the betel nut?" Lei whispered to Qing. She had never been around someone who had this habit.

"Yes, but it's not really the betel nut, it's the seed from the areca palm. It is wrapped in a betel leaf. My family will be sure to offer you some when we arrive. Don't be afraid to take some. It has a peppery taste and will relax you."

"Maybe," responded Lei. She would have to think about this. She wondered if it would affect her developing baby but didn't want to ask. Qing had been very talkative on the train about the coming baby. She already had a way of talking about it as if it truly was she who was pregnant. Maybe she's practicing so her friends will believe her, Lei had consoled herself. Lei knew Qing was going to have to tell her mother the truth but she wasn't sure about the other family members. Would this brother find out?

They passed billboards advertising holiday resorts across the island. Lei had never seen so many trees, not just spruce and fir, but also rainforest trees such as palm trees and the kapok tree, known for its silk-like fibre. They passed pineapple plantations and stands of coconut trees as well as bamboo. Stalls filled with colourful, local fruits and vegetables drew attention to settlements of indigenous people.

"I wonder if we will see a leopard?" Lei asked Qing. "I heard they are almost extinct now.

"You'd be pretty lucky if you did. Open the window though and you should be able to hear the gibbons high on the mountain ridges."

"I can! They're hooting away. Will we go past them?" Lei asked, directing her question at Bo.

"You never know your luck." He answered, obviously having learned this phrase from the tourists. "Let's get something to eat." Qing's brother said as he swerved into a spot in front of a food stall.

Qing took her hand and led her past the stall and into a compound behind the stalls. "This is my Aunty's home."

A hunched little woman, almost dwarf-like, emerged

from the opening in the centre of the wooden house. When she spotted Qing, her grave face lit up with a smile. She must have been about seventy years of age. Her smile showed missing teeth and the stain of betel juice. Her rough hands, pulled at the long pleated skirt she wore. Embroidered butterflies in brilliant silk threads fluttered over her blue hemp blouse. Silver jewelry shone on her wrists and neck. She was fair skinned. Qing had told her that many of the Miao people had fair complexions and even had blue eyes. Research said they originated as Caucasians migrating from Mesopotamia after the fall of the tower of Babel in Biblical times. Lei didn't know anything about this and it had sounded a bit far fetched, but now that she saw Qing's aunty she could see that it might be true.

Three toddlers dressed for winter weather followed Qing's aunty. They were bundled with layer upon layer of clothing, in contrast to Aunty's light clothing. Aunty bent to wipe one of their noses with the fabric of her skirt. When she looked up she included Lei along with Qing in her welcoming smile.

"Qing, my favourite niece. What brings you home at this time of the year? It isn't Spring Festival yet."

"No, I have some better news, Aunty. I will have a baby son soon."

She stepped forward and attempted to stroke Qing's belly. "It is overdue. Your family will be pleased. Qing backed away, but smiled to make up for her reservation.

Lei was puzzled. Why has Qing told them the lie? she questioned. Dageng had said to keep it a secret, until they knew if the baby was a boy.

"This is my sister-in-law, Lei." Qing said, looking around cautiously to be sure no one was nearby and could hear them. "She is the one who will birth my baby. We will need your help to find a doctor who will sign the birth register for me."

The hands of the old lady dropped from Qing's. She extended them to Lei, gripping both of Lei's hands in hers. "Of course I will help," she said. Her hands moved to caress Lei's belly. "A baby is a treasure and something to be valued," she said enthusiastically, quoting the Confucius saying.

"Why can't you keep it?" The old woman's bright gaze seemed to penetrate Lei's face looking for an answer. Tears welled up in Lei's eyes.

The old woman stared a moment and then said,

"Never mind. You must have your reasons. Best to keep them to yourself. The walls have ears you know."

"We need to know if it is a girl or boy," said Qing.

"I thought you already knew."

"No, I just want it to be a boy because Dageng will only let me keep it if it's a boy."

"You know it is dangerous to find this out. It is now against the law. Dageng is a fool to think this way," Aunty said as she spit some betel juice in disgust. The juice hit the ground so hard that it created a little dust cloud. The toddlers came to investigate the little purple puddle.

"Will you help us, Aunty?" asked Qing.

"Yes, but it must be done in secret. I will visit you at your mother's house when I find a doctor willing to do it. Tell no one of your situation, Qing. We are lucky as Miao people but Lei is not."

# CHAPTER 31

Back inside the three wheeled truck, Qing and Lei slept the rest of the way to Sanya, their heads resting together as they bounced along.

Qing's brother eventually stopped in front of a tall walled compound draped with budding wisteria. Wicker cages of small birds hung on the gateway to the courtyard.

The family home was set in a neighbourhood amongst other three-storey homes, each with walls and gates around them. Many had barking dogs behind their gates. The roads connecting them were unpaved. The highway they had been on led to the beach resorts on the south shore of Hainan.

"Did you know we call this island the Hawaii of

China?" Bo asked Lei,

"No, never heard that," she responded.

"Yes, the beach sand is white and the sea surf is rolling." He unlocked the gate and went through to an open sliding door. He set their packs inside. Seconds later, Qing's mother emerged.

"Qing, I am so happy to see you. Are you well?"

"Yes mother, I will tell you why we have come after we eat."

"Your father will be home soon. Sit. Who is this with you?"

"It is my sister-in-law, Lei. She is married to Dageng's brother Yimin. You have never met him but he is very kind. So is Lei."

"Come Lei, come and sit till Qing's father comes home. You look flushed. Are you well?"

"Yes, she is well Mother. She is just in a condition."

"What do you mean, 'a condition'?"

Qing knew her brother had left to go to the market so she felt safe to share their story with her mother.

"She is pregnant, but she and Yimin have agreed to give the baby to me and Dageng."

Lei's heart jumped as she heard these words coming

from Qing. The reality of her decision now out in the open.

"Why would you do that?"

Her unrelenting gaze demanded an answer from Lei. Before Lei had time to answer, Qing spoke. "Because she already has a child."

Lei knew immediately that Qing's mother did not approve of this plan. Qing rushed on, determined to share everything with her mother. "Dageng agreed to this plan because I still cannot get pregnant. Surely you and father will be pleased?"

"Why would we be pleased by your brother-in-law's child? Can't you wait a little longer to have your own?" her mother questioned. Her eyes searching Lei's body for signs of pregnancy. Lei was tempted to raise her loose tunic and show her tiny bump in her belly, just to validate herself.

"I don't want to wait longer," Qing averred. "It's been seven years." She reached for a tissue to stop the tears that were forming. I might have another girl. This plan will help Yimin and Lei keep their child," she continued. "Lei doesn't want an abortion."

"Perhaps she has to. It is the law for her," Qing's

mother said harshly.

Lei twisted her fingers in her cropped hair. She had thought Qing's mother would be happy for her daughter to finally have a child. She never thought she would resist their plan.

"I am going to keep it," said Qing defiantly. "Even if it is a girl, I will keep it. Dageng's parents are going to talk to him about keeping a girl. It is time for us to have a child."

The woman studied her daughter, saying nothing for several moments. Lei held her breath, knowing the fate of her baby was in this woman's hands.

Qing's mother moved to sit beside Qing, and her face softened. She looked from one woman to the other before she spoke. "If this is what you want Qing, I will agree." She coughed as if having a hard time finding the right words. "Yimin is family. We are all one. If you and Lei have agreed, I will help you both."

She paused a moment. "But how will you do this without being found out?"

"Lei and I have already planned it. I will dress like I am pregnant, and Lei can hide her belly. When the time comes to deliver the baby, Aunty in Haikou said she would arrange a doctor who will do the delivery and sign the registration papers. We can tell others that Lei is a midwife and wants to be with me at the delivery."

"That should work," her mother agreed, but you will have to be careful. People are nosy here. Our neighbours will wonder why you brought your sister-in-law to our community. You are right, if we tell them she is a midwife, they will surely accept that. We must plan this very carefully. Don't talk to anyone about your plans. Let me share your news."

There was silence as Qing and Lei realized the precariousness of their situation. Qing's mother now smiled at Lei as she busied herself filling the thermoses of hot water that the women would use to wash up before eating. She felt more like one of the family as Qing's mother handed her a thermos.

When Qing's father arrived, her mother told him the news, telling him that it was Qing who was pregnant. He was pleased, already anticipating that she would give them the long awaited grandson.

Once everyone was fed, Qing's mother said, "Go to bed now, you both need rest."

Lei lay on her new bed. So this was where she would live

for the next six months. Could she really hide her pregnancy from everyone? Wouldn't her joy show in her face? She massaged her belly gently, sending waves of love to this new little one. She at last felt safe. She rolled onto her belly and let her mind drift back to her first pregnancy.

She tried to recall the mystery of Kai's growth inside her. She had taught school right up until the last week before he was born. She had been busy with work rather than days of wonderment about the baby.

She finally fell asleep, the feeling of contentment soothing her whole body into relaxation.

Lei awoke hours later from a nightmare. Qing and Dageng were pulling on her legs. They were fighting over the baby. Dageng's voice was very clear. It's a girl, Qing. You must get rid of it.

# CHAPTER 32

When Dageng had returned home from taking Qing to the train, he found his parents both waiting for him. "Why are you not working?" he asked them.

"Sit, son. And have some tea with us."

"I need to go and finish the rice planting."

"Sit," said his father more firmly. "It won't take long."

Dageng took off his outer clothing and sat on a small stool.

The tea kettle was stuffed with green tea. His father poured boiling water over it, ensuring it brewed properly. Minutes passed and then his mother poured them each a small cupful.

They drank in silence. His mother poured them each another cup.

"Your mother has told me of this plan you and Yimin have agreed upon."

"Yes, father."

"We think it is a good plan. It is time you had your own child."

"I will only keep it if it is a boy."

"We think that is foolish, Dageng. You and Qing are allowed another child after this one and that one might be a boy. This one is already formed. Take it, whatever sex it is."

"No, it must be a boy, or we will wait until we have a son of our own."

"But what if yours is a girl, Dageng?" his mother asked as she poured them a third cup of tea. "Will you make her destroy it again?" she asked cruelly.

"We will have a test and make sure it is a boy."

"Dageng, are you forgetting, Qing has not become pregnant in seven years. She may be barren."

"We will wait. I want a son."

His father spoke up, anger in his voice. "Son, our

family is already blessed with Kai, let us look to the next one as a treasure."

"It will not be your child," he said looking them both straight in the eyes. "It's ours." He stood to leave. "We will wait for a son. Yimin has a son and I will soon have one. I will write Qing and remind her she must respect my decision."

His mother spoke next. "Do what you must Dageng, but we think you are wrong."

Dageng turned and headed for the door. His mother cleared the cups and called to Kai. They followed Dageng who was angrily pushing his wheelbarrow to the fields.

Kai's grandfather gave him a ride in the rickety wheelbarrow. Kai waved to his uncle as they passed him on the raised canal between the fields, but Dageng did not wave back.

# CHAPTER 33

Lei's father sat amongst his herbs and the medical records he had managed to salvage from the rubble the night his things were vandalized. Some still showed signs of being scorched from the fire.

"Will they come back?' his wife asked as she entered his small consulting shed.

"If they do, we will have to allow them to see we have nothing to hide. Lei has gone now and they have no proof of her pregnancy. We will tell them she has gone to be with her sister-in-law who is pregnant."

"But Dageng wants to keep it a secret till after they are sure the baby is a boy."

"It's too late now, Yimin told his employer that it wasn't Lei that was pregnant but Qing. They told Gang.

She cannot do anything about this because Qing doesn't need a birth permit. The men at the hospital are saying that Gang has been punished by her parents for not giving them our money. Gang denies having it. The officials told me they will return our money but I don't believe them. I think she's got it hidden somewhere with all the other dirty money she collects from women."

"Be careful what you say, my husband. Careless talk costs lives."

# CHAPTER 34

The moon shone through the open window of Ian's small flat. Cezanne lay nude beside him, the heat of their passion still warm on her flesh.

"I can't leave tomorrow," she stated. "I must try to follow Lei."

"You have to leave. To resist will cause trouble for her and Yimin." He cradled her in his arms.

"When you get home you can go to the Chinese embassy and try to get a re-entry visa. Tell your story to the Canadian consulate. I doubt they will give it to you though. It may be a long time until you are allowed to return to China."

Ian shifted his weight, allowing Cezanne to snuggle closer to him.

"What will you do?"

"My company wants me to stay as long as I can. Since Gang's release, her parents are trying to implicate me in a foreign corruption scheme. My company will probably move me out of the area. They may send me to Tianjin. We protect many overseas vessels that trade from that seaport."

"Couldn't I go with you? Then I could take a flight to Hong Kong and then to Hainan?"

"You couldn't buy the plane tickets. Your student visa has been cancelled." They lay in each other's arms, the futility of their situation painfully obvious,

"What's that noise?"

"It's someone at the door. Stay here, I'll get it." Ian pulled a pair of pants on and pulled a t-shirt over his head. The knocking on the door got louder.

"Get dressed," he told Cezanne.

Unbolting the lock on the inner door, Ian slid the peep-hole cover on the outer door aside. "Who are you?" he demanded.

"Open up and we will show you."

Aware of Cezanne's presence in the other room, Ian hesitated. "Tell me what you want."

"Open now or we will get someone to break this lock."

"Okay, okay, what do you want?" he said as he opened the door.

Two thugs pushed into the room. Their size made Ian look like a stick man. Within minutes, one of them had twisted his arm behind his back, allowing the other man to kick him in the groin and punch his face. When the man released him to slump to the floor, Cezanne ran from the bedroom, a robe over her body. She covered Ian's body with hers.

"Get up," the intruders shouted. "Or you will be next."

"No, leave her alone," Ian managed to say through his bloody mouth.

"Pack your stuff, you are leaving tonight."

"Leaving for where?"

"It doesn't matter. Now move, before we work you over again."

Ian stood, wiping the blood from his face with the back of his hand. "Get your things Cezanne and go quickly. Be sure to be on that plane tomorrow. These people mean business." He held her close a moment before he released her and pushed her back towards the bedroom.

Cezanne did as she was told, gathering her things and slipping silently out the back door. She heard the slam of the front door as they left for the street in front. She knew they had Ian with them. The alley way was still dark. She flagged a pedicab and directed it to her university dormitory. Her heart beat frantically. Would Ian be safe? She wanted to go straight to the Canadian Embassy but she was afraid that it could make things worse. She had heard rumours of cases where embassies had been forced to hand their nationals over to the Chinese police. She was pretty sure that they could use her as a tool against Yimin and Lei.

"Just do what they say," she heard Ian's voice tell her.

She had been given a day to leave the country, and she knew that obeying was the only way she could help her friends now.

Packing her things in one small suitcase, Cezanne reran the previous day in her head. The immigration officers had escorted her to the administration office. They had presented her with a one way China Airline ticket to Vancouver. When they told her she would be unable to complete her Masters Degree in the Peoples Republic of China she had asked to phone the Canadian Embassy but they wouldn't allow it.

"If you know what is good for you, you will do as we say. A car will pick you up at 8 a.m. tomorrow morning. Be ready. Talk to no one about this."

Cezanne closed her suitcase and sat on the bed. She had five hours till her plane left. She tried calling Lei but there was no answer. She tried texting her but it bounced back. "Receiver out of the network area," it said. What could that mean?

# CHAPTER 35

The soft sound of someone playing a reed pipe drifted down from the mountain terraces above Qing's family garden plot. A peacock strutted up and down between the rows of vegetables.

"Here's a letter for you, Qing," her aunt said as she arrived with her husband. Aunty sat on a board seat set in her husband's garden cart. He steadied the cart, his leg resting on the ground as he straddled his bicycle.

"Thanks Aunty, I can see it is from Dageng."

"Stop and rest and read it," her uncle advised.

"What does he say?" asked Lei, stopping her weeding as well. "Does he have news of Yimin?"

"No, it is very short. He is just reminding me that we must have the baby's sex determined before we agree to take the child and he says it must be a boy or I cannot keep it."

Qing held back her tears. She tried to smile at Lei.

"Are you sure he really means it?" Lei asked as she stroked Qing's long hair, "Maybe his parents haven't spoken to him yet."

"I know Dageng, and he means it. He decided this long ago and he won't change. She turned to look at Lei with downcast eyes.

"If the baby is a girl, I cannot help you Lei."

Lei felt her throat close. She could say nothing. She drew in her belly muscles and felt the baby stir. She had hoped they wouldn't have to find out the baby's sex until delivery time. She was so sure once Qing saw the baby she would find some way to keep it, even if it was a girl. Now she would have to undergo the ultrasound.

Her heart was heavy as thoughts rushed through her mind.

What if it is a girl? What will I do? Qing can tell her friends and family that she had a miscarriage. But what about me? Where will I go? Lei bent to start pulling weeds again.

"I'm afraid to have the ultra sound," she said out loud.

"What if the doctor makes me have an abortion right then and there? I have heard of such things happening."

The girls worked side by side until dark. Neither spoke of the letter again.

The following day a letter came from Yimin. *I know that Dageng has written Qing,* it said. *He told me for sure he will not keep the baby unless it is a boy. I think you should reconsider an abortion before they make you have one.*

Tears trickled down Lei's face as she read. Surely they had agreed they would find a way to keep this baby. Why had he changed? She read on, *Your family has suffered already because of your decision.*

What did he mean by this? What had happened? Why didn't he tell her how they had suffered?

She continued reading. *They denied you are pregnant even though Gang insists you are. She has no proof so if you can come home without the baby, all will be well. Gang's parents are determined to punish your parents because of the loss of face for them when Gang was charged with corruption and they got no money. Cezanne and Ian's visas have been cancelled and they were both made to leave China. I am sorry to tell you this news.*

He continued, *I am still not drinking, and am going to many meetings. Do not expect to see me at Spring festival. Gang watches*

*our family carefully. But I visit Kai every weekend, and he always
asks for you.*

Her tears flowed as she read to the end. She took the
letter and tucked it in her bra. She continued weeding.
She would read it again by the light of a candle, not once,
but many times.

# CHAPTER 36

Yimin stepped out from behind the parked Mercedes. The young girl opened the door, motioning for him to get in.

"No, Suzette, I told you we are finished. Now leave me alone."

"How can you say that?" she said as she pouted and flicked her long hair in his direction. "You know we have unfinished business. I told you I think I am pregnant. It can only be from you."

"And I told you to get rid of it. You're too young to have a child."

"No way, I want this child and I want you. You can have our protection at the factory if I can have your protection to have this baby. You only have to sign my birth permit."

"We're not even married, you would never get one," Yimin said as he reluctantly got into the passenger's seat. His body collapsed onto the padded leather.

Suzette immediately bounced over the gearshift and sat in the seat with him. Her slender body hardly took any room. Light from the street lamp shone through the windshield, glinting on her lipstick. Her hand reached to caress his thigh. He removed her hand.

"You're not listening Suzette. I can't get involved with you. I have problems of my own."

"If you mean with Gang, we can work that out for you. She counts on our protection too."

"Are you saying you could get my money back from her?"

"If that's what you want, I can," her hand went to his involuntary erection.

"Come with me. I have the key to my father's suite. He is away for a week."

Yimin sighed in defeat. At least alcohol wasn't involved he heard himself rationalize. "Just this once, Suzette, and then we are finished."

Suzette smiled as she slid back into the driver's seat.

Later, in the satin-sheeted bed, she murmured, "Don't talk Yimin, just stroke me."

In spite of himself, Yimin's hand went to the familiar part of her body. She had come back into his life as soon as Lei had left. In spite of his resistance they had spent almost every night together either in her father's suite or her car. If they weren't having sex, they were arguing about the new stance he was trying to take. No more alcohol and no more sex. Suzette ignored his words and was jealous of the time he spent with Kai or at AA meetings.

Yimin had tried to talk to his sponsor about his struggle but he seemed to think the meetings and no alcohol would sort everything out.

When their sex was finished, he broached the subject again. "I can arrange an abortion for you where no one will know you."

"No, I said I want to have this baby. I want you to look after me. If it is a girl it will be as pretty as me and if it's a boy it will look like you!"

"Don't you understand, I can't look after you. I have hardly enough money to look after my wife and son."

"If you work for my father, he will make sure you

have enough money."

"Your father would kill me if he knew I got you pregnant."

"No he wouldn't. He says he will take me away to America with him next time he goes. I could have the baby born there."

"If that is what you want, do it. But leave me out of it." Yimin dressed quickly and left her father's suite. He had a meeting to go to.

*****

"I am an alcoholic and I am proud of it." The member at the mike enunciated.

How can he be proud of it? Yimin asked himself. I haven't been able to accept the first step, which is trusting in a power greater than myself. What does that mean? Aren't I the one responsible for myself? Haven't I really messed up my life? Who could straighten that out for me?

"'Letting Go and Letting God', is one of the most powerful slogans," the speaker continued, interrupting Yimin's thoughts. Those around him were nodding their heads in agreement, as if they had had personal experiences with it themselves.

"Making amends is Step 4, and to do this you must truly be sorry for what you have done to others. Telling them you're sorry helps not only them, but also you. Remember only to do this with people who will not be hurt by your confessions," the speaker added. "If you can't apologize directly, you can stop doing the behaviour. This is another way of making amends."

That's where Suzette comes in, thought Yimin. She knows about Lei but how could I ever tell Lei about Suzette? How could she possibly forgive me for the result of that night under the influence of alcohol? Or now that we are still seeing each other. I can't blame it on the alcohol anymore. What is wrong with me? Why am I so weak around Suzette? I feel so strong about quitting drinking and I know I love Lei.

Yimin left the meeting before it ended. He couldn't work out what to do. It was that night he wrote another letter to Lei. *Lei, if you want this baby, I think we will have to divorce. It's the only way I can tell you about what has happened since you left. I am not worthy of your love. I will tell you why when you come back, but if you want our marriage to last, please come back alone.*

He never mailed the letter.

# CHAPTER 37

Spit, bang, spit, bang! Firecrackers exploded throughout the village to wake up the sleeping dragon who would bring the rain for the crops to grow. The Miao people traditionally believed in the Taoist Divine Goddess Nu Wa who is called the Mother of China. It was she who is believed to have separated the heavens and the earth and then proceeded to mold humans from clay to populate the world.

Lei heard herself saying, "Dearest Nu Wa, protect this next little human to be born to me." She sat huddled on her bed, her arm wrapped around her enlarged belly. Qing entered the room, the round pillow under her blouse making her look convincingly pregnant. Her mother said it wasn't necessary, that they could tell the family the truth, but Qing insisted because of her promise to Dageng and because they did have unexpected visitors dropping by, especially to look at Lei, their far northern Chinese relative. They wanted to see for themselves if it was true that Lei's features were different from theirs, and her skin darker.

Lei brushed aside her fears. Qing shared, "Tomorrow will be the ultrasound."

The two girls sat side by side looking out at the fireworks. Voices from below drifted up the stairwell to their room. There was a special gaiety this year because Qing was pregnant. Everyone wished for her to have a son and she assured them it would be. Last time she told someone this, she slyly winked at Lei, as if she expected Lei to know some way to make sure this baby was a boy.

They fell asleep together that night. Lei lay on her back with her arms above her head. She woke in the night to find Qing's arm resting on the bulge that was the new baby.

The next day the sun shone. There was no sign of rain from the gods. They were at a small backyard clinic in Haikou. Lei lay on the metal table. She was alone except for the voices of Qing and her mother talking outside.

Qing's Aunty had arranged this test now that she was in the fifth month.

"Pay him well," Aunty had said. "If it is a boy, he says he will be your delivering doctor and record Qing and Dageng as the parents as we have requested. If it's a girl, he's ready to do an abortion."

"No," Lei insisted. "I'm still going to find a way to keep her. My mind is made up."

Lei flashed back to the day she had talked with her mother about this situation. She was sure she would still be proud of her decision. Today she felt very strong.

The doctor entered the room, instructing her to lift her blouse, exposing her protruding belly. He smoothed the cold gel on her stomach, planted the instrument on the slippery surface of her skin. They both stared up at the monitor.

It was a miracle. This was her baby. She had never seen Kai at this stage.

The doctor moved the instrument around, pointing out the little head, arms and legs,

"There is no doubt, this baby is a girl." His voice was like a knife to Lei's heart.

"Are you sure?" she wanted to ask but he was already

wiping the gel from her belly with a towel.

"You should have an abortion from what Aunty has told me of your situation. I can do it now."

"No, not now." Lei moved quickly to get off the table. She reached down to pull her pants up protectively. "I'll come back if I decide to do that."

"Don't wait too long, if she gets much bigger we'll have to crush her skull to get her out."

Lei almost vomited. She leaned over grasping her belly.

"Are you alright?" the doctor asked. "Maybe you should get up on the table again. Today is the best day to do it."

"No. I will come back."

She heard the doctor telling Qing and Aunty the bad news. Qing started to cry and Aunty drew her to her breast to calm her.

"It's okay, Qing," Lei heard herself saying. "We can make Dageng change his mind when he sees her."

"No," Qing said through her tears. She pushed Lei away as she reached to console her. "Get away from me. I don't ever want to see you again!" She pulled the pillow from beneath her blouse and threw it at Lei.

"Stupid idea," she said as she rushed out the door. Her brother was waiting outside for her, a look of surprise on his face. She climbed inside the truck and he drove away, leaving Lei behind.

What can I do? Lei questioned in shock when she realized they were gone. "Where can I go?

"You can come to my home Lei," she heard Qing's Aunty say. "If we are very careful, no one but our Miao people will find out you are pregnant. I can deliver the baby for you and then we can decide what to do. I know the Han people say you must follow the law, but we are happy you don't. Any life from the gods is precious. You can stay until after the baby is born. Maybe we can find adoptive parents."

"No, I will never give her away to strangers. I will keep her somehow."

"There, there, don't think about it now. Come with me. But be careful. Hide your belly."

## CHAPTER 38

Lei was in shock as she drove back with Aunty on the wagon pulled by her mule. Her mind was numb.

Alone in the room Aunty gave her, she asked herself how she was going to manage. Thank goodness she still had the money Yimin gave her when she left. She worried that the money would be all used up before the baby was even born.

If only she could get a message to Yimin, she was sure he would help her even though the baby was a girl. He had promised to. Now she could tell him they would have a sister for Kai. He would be her big brother, the defender of her virtues. As her mother, Lei would teach her to cook and clean and would see that she got an education. Maybe one day the whole family would go overseas together. She wanted to tell Cezanne she would be an aunty.

You're crazy! her inner voice told her. You will be lucky if this baby lives. That doctor could still report you and insist you have an abortion. Maybe even Dageng's family will do that.

"Don't fret now child," Aunty said as she arrived with a stack of clean clothes and bedding. We won't go back to Qing's to get your things. They are likely to burn them."

"Here are two thermoses with warm water in them," she said after another trip downstairs. "Put them by the door when you finish with them and I will fill them up again. Rest now, you must be tired. I will make some soup to strengthen you. After lunch let's climb the mountain and find a tree to hang a bottle of wine in. This will please the gods and ensure your baby is safe."

Lei lay on her bed. She knew now that this baby relied on her to save it. Even more so, now that she knew it was a girl. But how? she wondered as she drifted into a fitful sleep.

# CHAPTER 39

Yimin walked from the AA meeting place to his dormitory. Suzette's car was parked in the parking lot, blocking his way to the building entrance. For a moment his heart skipped a beat. Had she brought her father to punish him for getting her pregnant?

Unable to walk around the car, he contemplated walking backwards and avoiding this encounter. Then the slogan, 'Let go and let God' came into his mind. He decided to trust a Higher Power's presence. He stood by the passenger doorway, unsure of what he would find behind the tinted windows.

Suzette lowered the window and whispered, "I've had the abortion like you wanted, Yimin." Her hands reached up to pull his head down to hers.

"Leave me alone, Suzette. I need to commit to my family. You have your father and the mother-in-laws. They will look after you."

Suzette opened her coat and flashed her low cut dress, but he was determined to be immune to her temptations. He had just accepted AA's first step. Yimin had admitted to himself and his sponsor that he was helpless and that his life had become unmanageable. Yimin needed help from a power greater than himself. He was determined to go to his parents and share his commitment to the program. He wanted to hold Kai close to his heart.

"Please Yimin, I don't care if I don't have your child, but I want you, no one else." Her face paled, covered with sheen of perspiration.

"Suzette, are you okay?"

"Yes, it's just the abortion. I'm still bleeding," she said as she slouched back into the seat, the streetlights accentuating her growing pallor.

"Let me take you to the clinic. You have to stop the bleeding. Move over, I'll drive." Visions of Lei's dangerous bleeding after her first abortion loomed in his mind.

Once at the clinic, Yimin stopped to attempt to help

Suzette out of the car. "Why did you stop here?" she muttered, a fresh set of perspiration forming on her forehead.

"Isn't this where you had the abortion?"

"No, my father arranged with a woman he knows to do it. She lives on the grounds of his factory. Please take me there."

Speeding into the traffic, Yimin worked his way to the gates of her father's ball-bearing factory. The guard on the driveway waved to the control guard to open the barrier once he saw that it was the owner's daughter in the car.

"Drive to the back entrance Yimin. The woman's shed is attached to the wall there."

Stopping at the door of the small shed, Yimin stepped out and knocked loudly on it. A stooped woman opened it and without looking at his face said, "It'll be 500 yuan no matter what month she's in."

"It's not about an abortion, woman. It's about one you've already done to the boss's daughter. Come and look at her, she's in her father's car." Suzette was slouched, barely conscious on the seat.

"Get her inside," the woman directed.

When Yimin struggled to lift her limp body, he felt the warmth of the wet blood through her dress. He followed the woman and laid her on the stained mattress on the floor. Looking around the cluttered room, Yimin swore. "Suzette, why would your father bring you here?"

"Shut up young man," the woman said. "Can't you see we might lose her? It's bad enough that the boss's daughter gets pregnant, now you want her to die?" The woman was removing some blood soaked padding from between Suzette's legs. "She just needs some new packing and some stronger medicine. Make some tea. There, by the sink. It will revive her."

Yimin did as he was told, holding the warm cup gently to Suzette's mouth. She smiled faintly at him as she tried to drink.

"Carry her back to the car and take her home. Don't bring her here again. If you have to, drive to another city and take her to a clinic. Her condition mustn't be found out by the Neighbourhood Committee. Her father's business may be corrupt, but his daughter must be pure. He has planned a future for her."

Driving Suzette home, Yimin realized again the mess he was making of other people's lives.

Wrapping her in quilts in her room, Yimin kissed her cheeks; colour was returning to them. "Your father will be home soon. I know he will take you to a doctor if you need to go again. Please understand I can't see you again."

Her hand slipped from his as she turned her face to the wall.

## CHAPTER 40

"Get out of here," Dageng yelled at Yimin as his brother parked his bike just inside the gate of their home. "It's your wife who has messed up our lives."

"What are you talking about?" Yimin held off his brother who was intent on wrestling with him.

"Qing is gone. She's gone back to Hainan. She was only here for 2 days. She left a note that she wants a divorce." Dageng's strength left him as he allowed his weight to lean against Yimin.

"What's going on?" their father asked as he emerged from the open doorway.

"It's Yimin. He didn't know about Qing leaving."

"You are both out of your minds," their father said. "Why can't you see that a baby is a treasure, not something to fight over?"

Not heeding his father's words, Dageng said, "You must write Lei and tell her to send Qing back to me. And she should get rid of the baby, Yimin," Dageng said. "You're both going to lose your jobs if she doesn't, and how will Mama and Papa manage now that you've lost all our savings?"

Their father stepped towards Dageng. His face red from the anger he was holding inside. "You shouldn't have been so pig headed, Dageng. Qing would make a wonderful mother. Now you have lost her. The only way you can win her back is for you to go and get her yourself."

"Never. She will have to come to me."

# CHAPTER 41

Aunty set the bowl of steaming rice between the little girls. Lei sat close beside them. A pet hare hopped onto the mat between them. The toddlers waited patiently for the fish and rice to be spooned into their mouths.

Since arriving at Aunty's house, Lei had taken on the responsibility of looking after the twins. They belonged to Auntie's sister who worked at the Miao Cultural Centre in Sanya. She and her husband left early every day to prepare the famous Miao five coloured rice dish to be served to the tourists. In the afternoon they participated in the bamboo raft dancing. The father played the lushing. He was one of the few men who still knew how to craft the instrument from six different sized reed pipes.

Antiphonal singing accompanied the flute players' music, initiating a connection with the spirit world. They also performed a circle dance where the single men played the music and the available woman danced around behind them, choosing their prospective suitors.

The children's mother left the compound every morning dressed in the elaborate costume of the Miao women, her silver headdress tinkling with shells and copper bells. Her husband, a silversmith, was proud of the intricate jewelry his wife wore around her neck, arms and ankles. This jewelry was part of the family's wealth and would be passed on to the little twins one day.

"Your weaving is improving, Lei." Aunty said as she held up the small woven hat Lei had made for one of the little girls.

"It is something I would never have learned in the city, Aunty. My friends will be surprised."

"What about your husband? Where is he?"

"He doesn't want me to bring home the baby. You know I am Han Chinese and I can't have another child unless we can pay for it. It is too late for that."

"Do you have your son yet?"

"Yes, he is four years old. You know Qing was going

to keep this baby for us but Dageng ruined that plan. I don't have another plan yet."

"Don't think about it now Lei. Keep your strength for the delivery. The gods will help you. Maybe I can find a local family who will keep the baby for you." She said this as she returned to her work at the treadle sewing machine set out in the courtyard of the compound. Every day until dark she worked on women's blouses with her machine embroidery. These blouses would be sold to the tourists at the beach.

Later, in bed, Lei questioned Aunty's use of the word "gods" and her plan to look for a local family to keep her baby. Did the gods really exist? Were they the same as the god her mother talked about? Could they really be called upon to help her? If only her mother were here to answer her questions. She was sure that together they would make a new plan, a plan that wouldn't involve giving the baby to strangers. Her belly was tight now, ready for delivery.

"Soon I will hold you little one," she said aloud as she cradled her belly in her arms and drifted off to sleep.

*****

The next morning Aunty entered her room just as the

sun was rising.

"Here's some tea, Lei. I know you are almost ready to deliver. I have some good news to share," she said as she set the tea down on the dresser beside Lei's bed.

"Qing's brother has told me Qing is arriving today. She has left her husband and plans to stay in Hainan, even get a divorce if she can."

What could this mean? Lei wondered. "Surely her family will send her back"

Lei wondered if she would see Qing again. She felt sure Qing would have news of Yimin.

*****

Lei woke later that morning to the gush of her water breaking.

"It's time," she called out. "Aunty, please come!"

Aunty arrived immediately and helped her walk to the clean room out the back, adjacent to the outhouse. Water was beginning to boil on the coal burner stove, and a clean sheet was already on the gang platform absorbing the warmth from beneath it. Lei crouched on the platform and began to moan, her arms curled around her bent legs. Aunty crouched beside her, massaging her lower back.

"Lean forward and push, Lei. She will come soon. It is your second."

Lei did as she was told, just four pushes and the head showed.

"She's coming, Lei, push harder." The twins' mother was also up on the gang, helping to balance her and bathe her face with cool cloths.

"She's beautiful," they said in unison as the infant emerged fully with the last push.

Aunty held out a towel that was quickly wrapped around the baby. They bathed her with warm water, and sponged off the clinging mucus and blood. Aunty cut the cord and tied it. A twisted cloth held it in place. There was no cry from the baby, but her eyes were wide with a light like no other Lei had ever seen. Their eyes met and it was as if they had known each other before. Had the gods given her back the baby she aborted two years ago? True or not, Lei held her close and guided her nipple into the baby's mouth. She suckled contentedly. Alive and well, thought Lei. Can this really be possible?

Lei drifted in and out of sleep as Aunty massaged the last bit of afterbirth from her womb. To this elderly little woman, Lei owed her life and the life of her daughter. If only..., she began to think, as she drifted off to sleep, her daughter resting safely in her arms.

# CHAPTER 42

Lei slept for hours. She awoke once and Aunty put the baby to her breast. They both fell asleep again.

In her dream, Yimin was there, holding the baby. He gave her the name *Wo Ai Ni*, I Love You, saying she looked like his lover. When Lei reached out to take the baby, they both faded away.

She sat up in bed, wet with the perspiration of her dream.

Her baby was gone. Aunty was there. She attempted to calm Lei. "It's better that you let her stay with my sister upstairs. She still has milk from the birth of her twins."

Aunty tried to calm Lei. "You must return soon to your family. It's better this way."

Lei attempted to stand, reaching back to the bed for support.

"I want to see her," she said as she headed for the stairs. Aunty saw that she was determined, so she supported her up the narrow passage. Inside the room she saw the baby was sleeping contentedly. The twins played peacefully beside her.

Lei gently lifted her into her arms, burying her face in the new baby's damp hair. There was a smell she remembered from when Kai was a baby.

"It's hot in here," she said as she used her nightdress to wipe the perspiration away from the baby's damp hair.

"What will you call her?" the sister asked.

"Xiao Yu," Lei said quickly. "Special rock. She is the treasure I once lost but now have found. I will call her Cezanne Siewling also after my Canadian friend and my mother."

"It's hard, I know, Lei, but you must let Aunty find a family to take her. Your family will call her a 'maggot in the rice', not a treasure."

"That's not true. My mother wants me to keep her," Lei responded defensively. "I thought my husband did too, but he has changed his mind." She stroked the newborn's head as if to reassure her that someone loved her.

Lei felt milk gush from her breasts, staining her nightdress.

The twins' mother said, "Go and let her feed. I will let her sleep with you until you leave. We can both nurse her so your milk won't come in too much. You must prepare yourself to return to your husband. Aunty has arranged for you to leave in three weeks."

Lei felt the warmth of Xiao Yu against her breast. She walked slowly down the stairs, her lips caressing Xiao Yu's tiny head. Her name Yu meant Jade, a valued stone in China. Cezanne can call you Jade, if she wants, she thought, but I will call you Xiao Yu, my cute and little one. Your name signifies purity, loyalty, sincerity. You are like the Miao divine Goddess Nu Wa that Aunty was telling me about. Maybe one day you will be powerful like the goddess and change things in China.

Sleep wouldn't come for Lei. She imagined leaving Xiao Yu in three weeks. Her hand stroked the fine hairs on her delicate head. She circled the soft spot, sensing the baby's vulnerability. Her fingers traced her nose. She gently opened the tight grip of her fingers. She felt the little fingers close on hers.

How can I leave you? Tears rolled down Lei's cheeks and onto Xiao Yu's arm. Lei knew that birds who were taken from their nests might never learn to sing the right song. How will you learn without me to sing to you?

Brushing away the tears that had landed on Xiao Yu's soft little flesh, Lei thought for a second of marking her skin somehow as some mothers do when they give their baby to an orphanage. How will I recognize you when I come back to get you? Her intent vanished immediately when she thought of scarring this perfect little creature.

She would have to trust. Was it a Higher Power she was trusting like Yimin had tried to explain to her?

The weeks passed quickly, each day bonding Lei more completely to Xiao Yu. The last morning Lei lay in bed with Xiao Yu as long as possible. She couldn't bear to leave her. With the infant sleeping contentedly beside her, she reached for her purse. She counted the money left. Yimin had given her a thousand yuan when she left with Qing on the train. It was almost all still there, Qing's family had asked for nothing for their hospitality. They had cared well for her until the day they abandoned her. Aunty had accepted a small amount to help buy food but had insisted that was enough.

When Aunty's sister came to her room an hour later, Lei was forced to give Xiao Yu to her. Unashamed tears rolled down her face as she followed the woman down the stairs and out into the sunshine. Aunty stepped in front of her as she made to follow, and led her instead to the kitchen where steaming hot congee was waiting for her.

"I'm sorry, I can't eat," Lei said as she left to go to her room.

They left her alone in her sorrow. Her mind was blank as she cried herself to sleep. She woke when the sun was overhead. Her breasts ached with the fullness of milk. Aunty's sister came into the room to bind her gently to stop the milk flow. They didn't speak but Lei felt her love.

Lei waited for Aunty to return from the fields mid afternoon. She was determined to work out a plan with her.

"I will leave you all my money, Aunty, and I will send you more, as soon as I am back at work. I must leave my studies and return to my job."

"Do as you wish daughter," Aunty said lovingly. "You

will need to save much if you are going to eventually get her back and educate two children. You will have to pay for her to have her own hukou so she can attend school."

Aunty continued, "In the meantime, I am sure the family I find will love her as their own. Miao people reverence all life. They would never harm her. She will be safe here until you can keep her."

Lei did not doubt her words. She had witnessed that in their community all the elders and toddlers were well-fed and cared for by their families. Many community members were involved with petitioning the government of Hainan to value their land and community for sustainability, rather than the export and profit that prevailed in the land since 1984 when the island was chosen along with nineteen other locations in China to be allowed to attract foreign investors. This was part of the Chinese politician and statesman, Deng Xiaoping's initiative. These towns and in this case the whole island, were meant to be guided by the ideals of socialism and yet allow the spirit of enterprise and capitalism. Democratic Socialism some people were calling it. Deng Xiaoping was quoted as saying, 'Do not care if the cat is black or white, what matters is it catches mice.' Some people also gave him credit for the saying, "To get rich is glorious." Lei had listened intently to the elders talking of how devastating these policies were turning out to be to the farmers. They were competing with corporations using costly fertilizers and pesticides. They all feared for the next generation.

I must be strong now, Lei told herself. I know I have made the right decision. I will return home and help Mother and Father prove to Gang and her family that they were mistaken about my pregnancy. I must show them how strong I am.

But what about Qing? Does she know if I had an abortion or not? Is she really here on the island?

Lei drifted off to sleep, finding comfort when Aunty's sister brought the twins into bed with her. They snuggled down, one on each side. She imagined the little girl was Xiao Yu. The little boy played with the new necklace she wore. It was a gift from Aunty of Chinese jade, entwined in silver strands her husband had made. To Lei it was a promise of getting Xiao Yu back one day.

## CHAPTER 43

The next day, Lei was surprised to see Qing arrive at the gate of the compound.

"May I speak with you Lei? Qing asked timidly before she paid the taxi driver. They both recalled their last parting.

"Of course, what do you want?"

"I want to say how sorry I am. I've left Dageng and plan to make a life of my own back here in Hainan. My brother and his wife have said I can live with them and I want to look after your baby. My brother told me it was born yesterday,"

"How did he know that?" Lei asked suspiciously.

"Remember, the walls have ears in China, Lei. It doesn't matter how he found out, but I am so happy because you know I wanted to help you whether the baby was a girl or a boy. I thought I could change Dageng's mind when I returned to Cixi but all I could see was his pigheadedness. He really is mean and unreasonable."

"What did Yimin say when you told him it was a girl?"

"He said he knew, and was counting on you to make the right decision. I think he is fearful of losing his job, Lei. How can you look after his parents and your parents if Yimin and you lose your jobs? That's why I want to help you. I promise I will tell the baby the truth one day." She paused to take a breath. "Where is she?"

"Here she is," Aunty's sister said, appearing suddenly with the little one strapped on her back in the embroidered Miao baby carrier.

Before Lei could lift the baby out, Qing removed the carrier and lifted the new little one out of it. She held her tightly to her chest. "You are beautiful," she said, covering her forehead with kisses. Xiao Yu stirred in her arms.

Lei felt a pain in her breasts as they filled with milk in spite of the bindings meant to suppress it. Ignoring the feeling, she stepped forward with the intent to take Xiao

Yu from Qing.

Instead, she said, "Are you sure you want to go through with this?" "What if your parents make you go back to Dageng? You were happy living in a big city. Are you sure you will be happy back here on this small island?" Suspicion showed in Lei's voice.

"No, I have thought it out carefully. I may never be able to have a child of my own. Xiao Yu will always be part of our family. Dageng was mean to insist I get rid of our first daughter and that we wait until I have a son. My brother thinks he will change his mind if I just show him your new little one," she said optimistically. "Maybe I can bring her to Cixi sooner than you think. What did you call her?"

"Xiao Yu."

"You are a valuable gem," Qing said. "I will trade you for my wedding ring. It was the only thing Dageng could buy me when his parents insisted we have a 'naked wedding'. Do you remember how mad he was?" she paused, her mind going back to those days.

"They insisted all the money should be saved for Yimin's education and we should announce our wedding as a 'naked one' as the saying goes. No celebration, no expenditures."

Lei shifted on her feet restlessly. She was too distracted to pay attention to what Qing was saying. She knew she would feel like this no matter who held her Xiao Yu. I want her, Lei's heart cried out, and she reached to take Xiao Yu from Qing.

Qing gently gave her to Lei, both women fussing over Xiao Yu's plump little cheeks.

"If you really mean what you say, Qing, I think it could work. But do you think you will be able to give her up when Yimin and I are able to keep her one day?"

Qing paused a moment before answering. It was as if she projected herself to that tragic day when Xiao Yu would find out she was only her Aunty, not her mother. As if resolved to tell the truth but at the same time determined to wait and face that day when it came, Qing responded quickly, "Of course, Lei. She will always be yours."

"I will need money to support her though, Lei. I didn't dare ask Dageng for money when I left. I had just enough money for the return train and ferry. I only left him a note about my decision."

Aunty interrupted their talking to say that she had

overheard them. She thought Qing had made the best decision and she told her that she was prepared to help Qing look after Xiao Yu if Qing wanted to work on their land.

"Surely you have learned some new technology since you left the island and worked with Dageng and his father? You will be an asset to us all."

"Most of it I learned from Yimin, Aunty. He is the one who studied agriculture at the University. He is always telling us new things to do to increase our crops."

"Yes, your Papa is a smart man, Xiao Yu." Lei heard herself saying to her little bundle.

"Did he tell you to tell me anything, Qing?"

"No, he didn't know I was going to leave. I think he still hoped you would decide to have the abortion.

Lei started to speak, then held back her words. I wish I could talk to Qing like I can to Mom and Cezanne. What is it about me that makes me hold back,  to tell myself I am of no value?  If only Mama or Cezanne were here, they would understand my turmoil.

Leaving the following week was not easy for Lei. She had spent almost every moment with Xiao Yu and Qing.

Many times Lei wished Qing would go and leave her

alone with Xiao Yu but she knew it was best this way. She even made herself leave the two of them alone and go for short walks. Aunty didn't approve of these walks. She wanted her to follow the Chinese custom of "lying in".

"It's bad enough you will leave within three weeks," she had said. "For your health Lei, you must follow the wisdom of your elders."

She wouldn't allow Lei to shower or wash her hair, not even brush her teeth.

"Do you want to get *yue zi bing*?" she asked, not waiting for an answer. "Our neighbour is very sick now in her old age and she knows her illness is from not following the Chinese postpartum routines after delivery of her babies."

Aunty insisted she keep warm and fed her on all types of different soups, alternating between fish soups and meat bones soup. Both were meant to enhance her breast milk. Her drinks were made with licorice and dried ginger roots as well as the white peony root. Most of her milk was drying up now as she nursed less and less.

Aunty suggested she go with Qing to see where Xiao Yu and Qing would be living. They walked to the nearby compound.

Qing's brother's compound was huge with ample room for Qing and Xiao Yu. His wife stayed at home with the children while her husband worked in the fields and market. Lei's heart stopped again when Qing allowed the young mother to hold Xiao Yu. She had to turn away and hide the tears that streamed down her face. Inside she knew her baby would be loved as their own.

The next day Lei had time to get a small silver bracelet from Aunty's sister's husband, as well as a small breast plate silver necklace that was traditionally worn by Miao girl babies. She had it inscribed with "Love you forever, Mama." She wanted to add Papa but she was still uncertain as to how he was going to react when she came home.

Leaving day arrived, and Lei handed over the necklace. "I will send you money, Qing. Watch for it at the beginning of every month. Write me if it doesn't come. The post is not always safe. I will try to come next summer, and hopefully Yimin and Kai can meet Xiao Yu then."

Before getting out of the wagon at the train station, Lei kissed the sleeping Xiao Yu and passed her to Qing's waiting arms.

"I love you Xiao Yu," Lei said as she gave her precious bundle to Qing. Once out, she turned to Qing in the front seat, "Remember Qing, I am her real mother."

\*\*\*\*\*

Yimin met Lei at the train station in Cixi. Wang was with him. They had just attended an AA meeting. Yimin stepped forward to embrace her, but she was rigid, resisting him.

Noticing this, Wang spoke up. "Your husband has made a commitment to the AA program, Lei. You have nothing to fear. Trust him now that you are home."

"Are you well?" Yimin asked, sincerity in his voice.

"Yes. I have done what I needed to do. Did Qing tell you what happened?"

"Yes, she said she advised you to have the abortion but you refused. I knew you would."

"Do your parents understand?"

"Yes, they are angry at Dageng. They were shocked to find that Qing had returned to Hainan. Did she contact you before you left?"

"Yes, she has our baby."

The surprise on Yimin's face confirmed that he knew nothing of this latest development.

"But what about her family? I thought they wanted a boy?"

"No, they are Miao and love all children. They were just trying to respect their son-in-law's wishes. They are growing to love Xiao Yu as their own.

"Xiao Yu? Is that what you called her?"

"Yes, I thought it was a perfect name."

Wang interrupted their talking, to suggest they catch a pedicab and go for dinner. "After all, we have much to celebrate," he said. "Yimin is a new father and he is celebrating his eight months of sobriety."

Yimin put his arms around Lei. "And Lei is a new and courageous mother. I am proud of her."

Once inside the pedicab, Lei asked, "Where is Kai?"

"He is with your parents. They wanted to keep him until you returned."

# CHAPTER 44

It was dark when they arrived at Lei's family home. The dogs didn't bark as they recognized it was Yimin and Lei. They let themselves in with Lei's key and crept up the stairs to her mother's bedroom.

"He's been waiting for you," her mother said as she passed the sleeping Kai to Lei. "Take him now and sleep. You've been through a lot. We'll talk in the morning." Her mother's hand squeezed hers.

Once Kai was settled, Lei turned to Yimin. She could tell he was feeling amorous, but she felt weak from the recent delivery and long train ride. Diverting his attention, she asked, "What about your young girl, Yimin? Is it over?"

"Yes, I am sure she will not bother me again. Her

father has sent her to America to study. She is young and has a promising future. He is rich and can give her whatever she wants."

"What if she wants you again and comes back?"

"Lei, I promise you I have learned my lesson. I am doing Step 4 now of the AA program and I am making amends with everyone I have harmed. I have promised her father I will never see her again. I know my love is for you and Kai and now Xiao Yu. Please forgive me for my unfaithfulness. I am sorry I let you down when you needed me the most," he said in a soft voice. "Actually I let myself down too. I will never do that again. Please forgive me and trust me."

Lei hesitated a moment before responding. She knew she had been forced to make her decision to keep Xiao Yu alone. She knew she was stronger now just by the act of having made it and having lived through it. Was she now going to let Yimin's affair set her back? Would she be able to forget the pain of his unfaithfulness? Could she trust him again?

Lei took a deep breath and exhaled, releasing her tension and giving her a moment to think. She knew if she wanted to keep the family together she was going to have to trust Yimin as she had trusted Qing.

Lei was suddenly aware of the beating of her heart within her chest. She heard herself saying, "Yes, Yimin, I forgive you." She knew she meant it.

# CHAPTER 45

The family awoke the next day to Gang and her group pounding on their door.

"We know you are in there, Lei. You are going to confess everything you have done, or I am going to destroy your family."

Yimin opened the door slightly, only to have it pushed fully open as the group moved into the sitting room.

Lei's mother and father emerged from the kitchen area and stood protectively beside Lei.

"You'll what?" said her mother. Her eyes didn't leave Gang.

"Just what I said," said Gang. "My father can destroy your husband's career and your daughter and son-in-law's jobs. He's ready to do it. We have just been waiting for Lei to come back. It's almost nine months since she left. We know she has given birth. Where is the baby?"

"Why?" said her mother. "Do you want to sell it?"

"What do you mean?" Gang said, a stutter in her speech.

"You know what I mean, and if you don't get out of here and leave us alone, I am going to the authorities. And not the local ones, they're in on it too. I'll go to Beijing. I have time to wait and be seen by the appeal court."

Gang shifted slightly in her position between the family and the door, her group looking to her for direction. "We will leave," she said.

She struggled to step over the track of the sliding door. Her eyes drilled into Yimin. "The mother-in-laws will be watching you, Yimin. You better make sure your wife obeys the law from now on."

"And we will be watching you," Lei's mother said as she stepped forward, her husband vainly attempting to pull her back. "You better stop your racketeering of babies immediately or we will have the central government authorities after you. Just because you couldn't keep your baby, you don't have to go on punishing others. I thought we made a deal you would leave us alone now that you know where he is."

Gang didn't answer. She just gestured to her group and they all left the compound with the two dogs snapping at their heels.

*****

The day passed with everyone eating and drinking together. Neighbours came to hear more of the story. Where was Qing? Where is the baby? Will you bring the child here one day?

Eventually her mother told them to go away.

"The walls have ears you know," she told them as they reluctantly made their way to their own compounds.

That evening, Lei sat on the bed to tuck Kai in. "Tonight I have a different bedtime story to tell you," she said as she pulled his quilt over his body and tucked it under him. She folded it back beneath his little feet. Snuggling down with both their heads on the feather pillow, Lei started her story.

"It's about a little baby called Xiao Yu." Her eyes met Yimin's as he looked on, lying close beside them. "You will meet her one day. Now she lives in Sanya with

Aunty Qing," she said as she tucked a loose strand of hair behind his ears.

"She looks just like you did when you were a baby but she's a girl. We will bring her here when she needs to go to school. You will both go to school together. You will be her big brother."

Yimin's hand caressed her shoulder as she kissed Kai on the forehead. Her mother looked into the bedroom as she passed in the hallway, pride in her eyes.

Lei heard a cough as her father entered the room. "I will help you Lei." He said with compassion.

Lei smiled, a look of pride on her face. "Our children will now be like the birds. They will always have their families to teach them *their* song."

## THE END

# ABOUT THE AUTHOR

Diane Bestwick spent almost a decade in China researching her novel. She was determined to write an authentic story, even though the characters are fictitious. She travelled extensively throughout China, living for short periods with many of her English student's families as well as in her teaching colleagues' homes.

Before embarking on her writing venture, she lived with her family aboard a historic sailing vessel, travelling in the South Pacific, and the Caribbean. Her first son was born in Fiji and her second son in Australia. She now lives on Vancouver Island, British Columbia, Canada. She is an advocate for the equality of women and plays a supportive role to several foster homes in China.

**You can visit Diane online at**
**www.dianebestwick.com**

Proceeds from this book help support foster homes in China. Thank you for your support!

Made in the USA
Charleston, SC
19 November 2014